Sweet
LIAR

LAURELIN PAIGE

Hot Alphas. Smart Women. Sexy Stories.

Copyright © 2019 by Laurelin Paige

All rights reserved.

No part of this book may be reproduced in any form or by any electronic or mechanical means, including information storage and retrieval systems, without written permission from the author, except for the use of brief quotations in a book review.

Editing: Erica Russikoff

Proofing: Michele Ficht

Cover: Laurelin Paige

Formatting: Alyssa Garcia

ISBN: 978-1-942835-53-0

Sweet LIAR

CHAPTER ONE

Dylan

"What the fuck was that?!" Weston, my business partner, exclaimed from the front passenger seat of my service car as we pulled away from the curb.

Restraining myself from directing the driver—a habit of mine, surely not useful now when I'd been out of New York City for so long—I looked behind me out the rear window at the two figures we'd left behind. Donovan Kincaid, another one of my partners at Reach, Inc. along with Weston King, was chasing down a girl who worked in the office—Sabrina Lind.

I had only just met Sabrina this evening. The woman was pleasant, smart, straightforward. Had a good head on her shoulders. Weston and I had dined with her and her younger sister and had just been finishing up when Donovan had come in, all blustering and noble and knightly.

"Donovan called himself her *boyfriend*," Weston said incredulously, recalling the scene we'd just left. "Was I the only one who heard that? I can't be *that* drunk."

It had been an out-of-character declaration for the usually tight-lipped and brooding Donovan, but I'd seen this side of him before, many years in the past. The last time he had given a woman his heart.

If anyone asked me, he was wasting his time with this one. Sabrina had said several things over dinner that suggested she was no longer entertained by the circus that surrounded romantic notions.

"I heard it," the young woman sitting next to me answered.

Now this one—Audrey, the younger sister whom I'd volunteered to see home—a man would have a much easier time trying to woo *her*. She'd made that clear over dinner as well.

Too bad she was *that* kind of girl. The kind of girl who wanted a man to love her before she lifted her skirt. Otherwise...

I turned my head slightly, imperceptibly, and slid my eyes down her form, pausing on the sweet curve of her breasts, watching her chest rise and fall with her breath. My gaze had traveled this journey several times this evening, but now I was lucky enough to have the added view of her legs, which had been hidden under the table before. They were long and toned, a little curve in just the right place.

"I heard it," she said again, "and it was *so* romantic."

The swoon in her voice made me chuckle. God, she was young. Younger than whatever ridiculous young age she actually was. Who the hell even believed in romance anymore?

"I don't understand," Weston muttered, combing his

hand through his hair. "I'm Donovan's best friend. I knew he was sleeping with her, but I didn't know he was her boyfriend. I didn't know he was *into* her. *I* was supposed to be into Sabrina. When did this happen? Where have I been?"

Oh. That was right. *Weston King* believed in love and relationships.

He turned his head to look at both of us in the backseat. "I'm seriously asking here."

I glanced at Audrey. Her expression said that she had been in the know, but her lips were sealed.

That left me to console my partner. "You've probably been too distracted with that Dyson pussy you've been banging," I was definitely still intoxicated. I didn't normally use such crass language in front of a lady. Especially such a *young* lady.

"Hey," Weston said, pointing a stern finger in my direction. "Elizabeth is not just some pussy I've been banging. I'm going to marry her."

Never mind that their engagement was part of a business ruse. Despite the fact that it counted for nothing, Weston seemed to have grown fond of the girl—even as he bemoaned the loss of Sabrina.

It was exhausting.

"You're exhausting," I told him.

"*I'm* exhausting?" He seemed baffled by the idea that he would exhaust anyone.

"The entire lot of you. More exhausting than the flight across the pond. All of you are intelligent creatures normally. I wouldn't have gotten into business with partners who gave in to the whims and fancies of human nature. It takes a clear head, your feet on the ground, your priorities straight, to be as successful as we have been with our company.

"But now the lot of you have gone and eaten some fruit from the tree of temptation. Drank the potion number nine. Watched one too many Netflix Christmas specials, because you've suddenly all descended into the ridiculous camp of men who fall in love with women."

"Wait," Weston halted me. "I never said I was in love with Elizabeth Dyson. I only said I was going to marry her."

"You spent the entire dinner pining after her. *Pining*, Weston King. Surely pining is a sign of love." I turned to the audience member that I knew would be on my side.

"Yes, indeed," Audrey nodded, with a bob of her head that was somehow both girlish and sexy as hell. "Pining is Love 101. If a girl came to me and said the guy had told her he was pining after her? That's like popping the question."

"Exactly like," I said straight-faced. I was being sarcastic, of course, but the girl did make me want to smile.

Among other things.

I stretched my arm across the back of the seat bench, casually, making myself comfortable. Not making a move. No, not that.

"I am not in love with Eliza—"

"And on top of your pining…" I said, speaking loudly over Weston. His denial, which he was surely about to deliver in full, was infuriating and, frankly, patronizing, and I refused to listen to more than a second of it. "We have Donovan, who declares a relationship with a woman on a public street, for crying out loud, in front of his partners.

I thought for sure that man, of all of you, had reason." He must have forgotten how miserable he'd been the last time he'd given his heart, albeit ten years ago.

Soon enough, he'd remember.

"And then we have Nate," I continued. A man of varied sexual pleasures and interests, Nathan Sinclair had been another fly I'd never expected to drop. "When I'd had drinks with the man last night, he was talking about one particular woman like she hung the moon. Soon it will just be me and Cade."

I leaned closer toward Audrey, since she probably didn't know anything about our fifth partner who headed the Tokyo office. "No one will ever love Cade, even if he goes pansy on us. That's a man that even a mother wouldn't love. He's one of my best friends. I ought to know."

Weston harrumphed from the front seat, completely indignant, but I noted a hint of optimism, as though he hoped I were right about his future, and that he'd be leaving the bachelor life for good.

He really had gone bananas over that Dyson girl. Poor sucker.

I stole another glance at Audrey, curious at how badly I'd offended her with my speech, love-cheerleader that she was.

But when I turned in her direction, I hadn't expected that she'd already be staring at me. The flush in her round cheeks as she looked quickly away sent a jolt to my todger.

I should have been ashamed of myself.

But I wasn't.

She was a very attractive young lady. I couldn't help how my body reacted. I'd been respectful. For the most part.

"This is me," Weston said, pointing out the window to his building.

My driver pulled over next to a large bank of snow. To be fair, the entire street was banked with snow, lingering from the storm the day before.

"Guess I'm going snowshoeing," Weston said with a sigh. He stepped out of the car and immediately cursed, the door slamming before I could make out the full extent of his blaspheme.

I leaned over Audrey, and not just because I wanted to smell the rose bouquet in her perfume, but so that I could roll the window down and call after my partner.

"Have a good Thanksgiving," I said, "if I don't see you again before the holiday." He was flying off somewhere later in the week—Utah or Kansas—the United States Midwest was always a blur to this Hampshire native.

"You too, friend. It was good seeing you. If even briefly. And nice meeting you, Audrey." He turned, stepping into the snow. "Fuck. These were a brand-new pair of Giacomettis."

"You can put them out with the rubbish, along with your balls. Since you're obviously not using *them* anymore." I rolled up the window before he could throw back a dig of his own, but he got me with a simple flip of the bird.

I sat back in my seat, accidentally grazing my hand along Audrey's bare knee.

Perhaps, not so accidentally, but I played it perfectly—the shocked drawback from the touch and an immediate apology, stammering so that she would indeed believe that the brush was innocent. With all the predators these days, I certainly didn't want to be confused for one.

Or at least I wanted to be my own breed of predator. The kind that knew when to behave. Though the shock of the touch had sent fire through my blood, it wouldn't be followed up with any pouncing.

We drove in silence for several minutes, a thick silence. Too thick. Too heavy, making the car hot and stuffy and tense.

I loosened my tie and stole another glance in her direction. She seemed to be lost in her own thoughts. Had I offended her after all with my touch?

Then I remembered the conversation from before Weston exited the car. That was more likely the cause of any hard feelings.

Normally, I would brush the whole thing off. Let her be offended. I wasn't changing my stance on romance to please her.

The tension between us, though, wouldn't dissipate. It seemed filled with more than just the words of what I had said. It was growing and breathing, and I felt the need to claw through it, the way you claw through bedsheets when they've twisted around you during a nightmare.

"You've been quiet," I said. Obvious. To the point. "Have I rained on your love parade?"

She twisted her head in my direction, her eyes catching a reflection of a streetlight making them spark in the darkness.

"You can't rain on my parade," she proclaimed with a smile, as though she were old Dolly herself. "I am firm in my faith." She swiveled a little more in her seat, angling herself so that her body was pointing in my direction. "Are you quite sure that you're firm in your disbelief?"

Heat traveled down my spine, liquid and molten. That's what this tension was, then—not of a disgruntled nature, but of the sexual. I'd been attracted to her, yes. I hadn't allowed myself to believe it might be mutual.

I studied her face. She had light almond eyes that were deep set in a pear-shaped face, her pallor flawless. Not a single line marred her skin. She was lovely. Delicious, I imagined. Fresh, like a peach. Her bee-stung lips, turned up on both sides below her apple cheeks, portrayed her as innocent.

I liked believing she was that innocent. It made it more fun to imagine what those lips could be taught. What they could be introduced to.

I'd sworn off love years ago, but not sex. Never sex. And Audrey Lind was all sorts of temptation, the kind I knew better to stay away from. She was too romantic. She was too American. She was too young. *Much* too young. I was definitely old enough to be her father. Probably.

Definitely.

I didn't want to think about that.

She was also the sister of a subordinate, which felt highly inappropriate, especially since I was only in town for the week. Donovan might have gotten involved with the staff, but at least he'd seemed serious about it. A fling was another thing altogether, not as polite.

And none of that mattered since she was so very young.

"You're hesitating," she said, her smile broadening as though she'd won some sort of trophy. "Are you unsure of your answer?"

I had to remind myself of the question. "No. My commitment to refute love and relationships in all forms remains unwavering." My eyes flickered to her plump lips.

The delectable mouth.

"I wonder if you're lying." Before I could offer a protest she went on. "Which isn't why I was quiet. I was thinking about Weston's situation. Not the current one, but how he was before he met Elizabeth. I'm normally not into players, but he's reformed. And his past has advantages."

Her words were a fishhook. If I were a smart little fishy I would swim away as fast as I could.

I was a smart fishy. I was.

But I liked to swim as close to the bait as possible. Just to see what it was.

"What exact benefits does Weston King have in being a former playboy who now thinks he's head over heels for a woman he's fake-engaged to? The first woman he's ever spent more than a weekend with, might I add." It was one of the messiest messes I had ever imagined.

"Well. Um." Her eyes fluttered downward and her cheeks darkened a bit. "Weston figured out what he was doing before he fell for Elizabeth. So when they were to-gether, it was...you know." She rubbed her lips together—believe me, I was watching everything she did with that mouth. "In the bedroom, I mean."

"Are you saying that you are not...? That you haven't...?" I cleared my throat, floundering a bit with how I was asking this near-stranger about her virginity. It was like the opening of a poorly written porno.

Holy mother of God, I was going to be fantasizing about this for quite some time.

"Oh, no," she said in a rush.

And to my relief. I couldn't handle the weight of know-ing that and later having to get out of the car to see her to the door of her apartment building.

"I'm not that innocent," she went on. "I've had boy-friends. Two serious. Long-term, each of them. Very committed, very in love with both of them. And, maybe, even, either one of them could have been the guy. You know, *The Guy*? The Forever Guy?"

The fairy tale. Yes, I knew that story.

She was in a car now with me though. Not *with me*, but she wasn't with anyone else either, from what I'd gathered during the night. So those fairy tales had obviously ended. The way that every fairy tale eventually does and life returns back to reality.

"So what happened?" I asked, guessing she was about to reveal the flaw in her religion.

"Our sex life happened. Or didn't happen. My friends used to tell me about all these filthy, hot, dirty things they were doing with their boyfriends. Really sexy, adventurous things. You know the way girls share everything. And my guys? Missionary. Every time. I swear to God. Once the boredom in the bedroom became obvious, it seeped elsewhere in our relationships. No matter how much I hinted or pushed to explore new things, my guys were always as ignorant as I am."

My trousers were suddenly much too tight. Oh, the things I could show her. The ways I could *be* with her. If every man had only ever been on top of her, rutting around inside like some horny little teenager—had she ever even had an orgasm? My body pulsed with the want to show her the sweetness of expertise.

But that couldn't happen. For all the reasons I'd gone through before. Whatever those reasons were. They had left my mind at the moment, but there had been many.

Good reasons.

Yet, even as I knew where this little car ride *couldn't* go, it seemed we were suddenly closer to each other. Audrey had unbuckled her seatbelt and smoothly slid across the bench toward me, and I hadn't even noticed.

I swallowed.

"I think your story of two men who could've been the one but ended up not, proves your theory of there *being a one* at all as flawed." My voice was still surprisingly steady. Fortunately. It didn't belie the pounding of my heart, the tingling of my skin. The rock hard state of my cock.

"No way. The One still exists. The theory isn't flawed. I had simply jumped to conclusions too soon. Maybe because I wanted it too much. Maybe because I wasn't ready yet. I still most definitely believe in kismet."

Her hand was on my thigh, like a hot iron burning through the material of my trousers to the skin underneath. It was a warning sign. A flash of silver threaded through a dead worm.

She lifted her delicate face up toward me, blinking her eyes innocently. "I'm pretty sure I can convince you kismet exists too, if you'll just do one thing."

Swim, fishy.

I didn't swim. "What's that?"

"Kiss me."

CHAPTER TWO

Audrey

"Kiss you?" he asked, and the wariness in his tone almost made me doubt myself.

Almost.

Actually, not even almost. More like, I wondered if I *should* doubt myself.

But I didn't. I didn't doubt myself at all. Why should I, really?

I'd always been confident. I'd had the good fortune of being raised first by a father who instilled power in me, and then an older sister who made sure I felt my worth. Ironically, Sabrina had often lacked faith in herself, probably because, as the oldest, she had felt the burden of filling the woman-of-the-household role at such an early age, our mother having died young and then our father only a handful of years later.

And, to be honest, mothering wasn't Sabrina's strong suit. It made sense that she struggled with her self-esteem, as she'd been thrown into that role when she'd never asked for it. I loved her grotesquely, exactly the way she was—strong, opinionated, and smart as hell—but she tended to be *too* strong for much of the traditional world. *Too* opinionated. *Too* smart. Weren't women supposed to be dainty and quiet and demure? Sabrina didn't buy into that, and I so very much appreciated her paving the way for me to walk behind her with my head held high, no matter what form of femininity I wore.

So I felt pretty secure with myself for the most part. I knew who I was—talented, but not quite talented enough to pursue a career based on selling my artwork. Smart enough to understand the chemistry and archeology that went into my nearly completed masters of art conservation. Attractive—no one would ever confuse me for a model, but I did turn heads. I certainly wasn't desperate. I got to choose who I paid attention to, and when I liked someone, I told him. I had no reason to play hard to get.

But even though I was fun and romantic, I never felt like I wasn't grounded or that I needed someone else to anchor me. I especially never needed a man for that.

Yet, I did *like* having a man in my life. When I had a boyfriend, the world spun around him. I was a love-with-the-whole-heart kind of gal. I didn't enjoy being alone, and never had. There's a comfort in knowing someone will always catch you when you fall that Sabrina had never been able to replace. I'd been single now going on five months. That had been purposeful. After the last relationship that had blossomed and thrived everywhere except the bedroom, I'd decided something had to change.

Finishing school, though, had been the priority, and I hadn't thought much about how I was going to bring about that change.

Until tonight.

Since I was visiting Sabrina in New York for Thanksgiving break, I'd intended to give her all my focus, not expecting that *her* head would be wrapped up in a guy. Not that I was resentful. She deserved some happiness.

Just…her preoccupation with Donovan left me free to, well, *notice*. Notice Sabrina's boss—the tall, sophisticated, much older Brit with the chiseled jaw and brown wavy hair. Notice the way his eyes melted like chocolate as he got more buzzed on wine. Notice how his gaze lingered on me throughout dinner, despite the two other people present. Notice the crackle and the spark of electricity that traveled between us.

Notice how he noticed me.

And, wow, was he fantastic to look at. And listen to. And be noticed by. It made me beam and pulse. A lot like when Mr. Gregori, my favorite art teacher, acknowledged my work in class. That was what Dylan felt like—a professor. A very sexy, very hot professor. The kind of professor who could teach a girl a thing or two. The dirty professor who obviously had naughty thoughts about his young student but was decent enough not to act on it. He let those thoughts simmer and stew instead.

It wasn't like any other attraction I'd felt before. There was no pretense. No expectation. Just this raw, primal interest drawing me to lean in, to angle my body toward him. Drawing me to be bold.

Drawing me to have Ideas.

"Yes, kiss me," I repeated, my hand on his thigh. I swear I could feel the temperature of his skin rising through his pants.

Still, he made no move to grant me my request.

"Am I supposed to fall in love?" he asked, studying me

with an intensity that made my heart beat against my ribs like a caged madman.

Gosh, he was noble. Wrestling with propriety even as his desire pressed against the wall he'd so firmly built around himself.

Or perhaps he feared that wall wasn't as sturdy as he proclaimed.

"Are you worried about it?" I challenged.

His eyes never left me. "Of course not."

"Then what are you afraid of?"

His restraint broke, and his mouth swooped down on mine like a wolf descending on its prey. There was no fore-play. No sweet seduction. Just hungry determination as he placed a hand at the back of my head and attacked with fierce ardor. He was firm and aggressive. He was skillful and demanding. He was in charge.

Silly, stupid, willing lamb that I was, I latched myself to him, throwing my arms around his neck and licking at the greedy plunge of his tongue between my lips. I wanted his taste of wine and smoked bass to be *my* taste, to be the only taste I could remember. I needed to drink him and devour him the way he seemed to need to drink and devour me.

We were frenzied and sloppy, our teeth crashing against each other at times, our breath coming in irregular mea-sures. It felt as though the whole of time had been reduced to this moment, the entirety of the universe reduced to the three square inches that belonged to his mouth, and even as existence was shrunk down to this tiny form, there was nothing missing. Everything, *everything* I could ever want or need or desire was found in the electric field of this kiss.

Soon, I became aware of more, my attention spreading

through my body like heat with the sunrise. My breasts felt heavy and my nipples tight. My belly swirled like a cyclone was tearing across its insides. Lower, between my legs, my core throbbed and ached. I was wet and empty, my thighs vibrating with need.

Desperate to ease the growing hum, to touch more of him and be touched, I swung my leg over his lap to straddle him and gasped when I landed on the steel ridge bulging from his pants. My hips bucked automatically, pressing my pussy against the outline of his cock. Again, again, needing to feel the exact shape of him, hoping to still the buzz that only seemed to grow louder with each stroke.

It was humiliating how eager I was. How urgent. How impetuous. How deeply romantic all of those things had suddenly become.

But then Dylan's hands were under my skirt, his fingers digging into my ass as he tilted my hips up along the length of him, deepening the notch of his cock, and I realized he was just as eager. Just as urgent. Just as impetuous.

And he knew what I needed. Knew exactly how to give it to me.

I felt myself get wetter. Felt him thicken against me. A frantic mewling sounded in my ears, and it took me several seconds to recognize it was coming from me. It was an entirely new and thrilling experience. Our lips stayed locked as we grinded and humped, a tight ball of tension growing deep in my belly. I'd never been so intimate with someone during a first kiss let alone the first night we'd met. Never felt so close to orgasm with all of my clothes still on. Never been on the verge of begging for sex from a near stranger—

The sound of a throat clearing brought me tumbling out of ecstasy.

Dylan broke his mouth from mine and peered around me. "Yes?"

The driver. Oh my God, I'd forgotten about our driver.

"This is the street," the forgotten driver said. "There's snow piled up against the curb. I've driven down the entire block, and there isn't a spot that's clear."

Dylan turned his head to look out the window, verifying the driver's claim. "Circle around the block, and let her off at the corner then," he said.

"Yes, sir."

The rhythmic click-click of the turn signal filled the silence.

My cheeks felt hot as I forced myself to meet Dylan's eyes. The need and urgency from only a moment ago still screamed between us, impossible to ignore even as my pulse began to settle.

Should I invite him up?

I wanted to.

But it was my sister's apartment. And he was my sister's boss, and there seemed to be a dozen things wrong with that situation.

Would he invite me to his hotel?

Also improper for as many reasons, and I saw from his expression that he'd gotten hold of himself enough to understand his obligations.

I shouldn't have felt so disappointed. I'd only meant for it to be a kiss. A kiss to find out if what I'd been considering was really something that might work.

Now I knew it could definitely work.

"You said I'd believe in kismet after that," Dylan said.

"Was something supposed to happen?"

I could have smacked him. Trying to play like I'd had zero effect on him when his cock was still as hard as stone underneath me.

Fortunately, I wasn't that easily deterred. "Yes. Now you give me your phone number."

He only hesitated for a fraction of a second before pulling out his cell phone and unlocking the screen. He handed it to me. "Text yourself."

I shivered. How could a person make something so innocent sound so naughty?

Because he was experienced, that was how. Because he knew things that I didn't. Because he was The Professor.

I quickly shot myself a text from his phone then handed it back just as the car came to a stop. "I'll talk to you tomorrow," I said, climbing off his lap.

And maybe because I'd moved too quickly, because I'd surprised him, or because he was curious, or maybe because he was hard and horny and not in his right mind, he didn't argue about my parting remark.

Instead he sat somewhat dazed as I slid across the backseat, opened the door, and disappeared into the night. I was dazed too, but I'd never been more confident in myself.

CHAPTER THREE

Dylan

I stared after Audrey, dumbfounded, as she walked to her building. My lips still burned from our kiss. My cock still ached and throbbed from her grinding on my lap. And I, like a fool, clung to her final words, "I'll talk to you tomorrow."

Fuck, how I wanted her to ring me. Wanted it like a teenage boy waited by his phone for the call from the pretty girl. The idea of it made me nervous and excited and... stupid.

That's what I was. Stupid.

Because even if she did ring me, there was no way I could accept her call, except to tell her that I was sorry for the egregious way I'd acted in the car.

Yet I *wasn't* sorry. Not truly. Not at all.

"Fantastic," my driver said dreamily, breaking my stupor.

I looked forward to find him also staring after Audrey.

Irritated, I scolded him. "What are you looking at?" He was even older than I was. It was inappropriate for *me* to be eyeing her. It was disgusting that *he* was. How I could feel both a fatherly protection and an indecent attraction to the girl, I had no idea.

That was a therapy session for another day.

"To the hotel, sir?" he said, moving his eyes back to the road where they belonged.

I didn't answer right away, staring at the mobile still in my hand. I'd had no texts from my son. When I'd seen him at lunch, I'd suggested we go out for a late movie tonight. He'd said he'd get back to me. I'd felt the sting of rejection, but he was thirteen now—independent and awkward. Moody, too. Even though I traveled across the ocean to see him, he wavered these days from wanting to see his dad and wanting to spend all his free time with his friends. I remembered this age. Remembered parenting this age. My stepdaughter, Amanda, had been thirteen when I'd married her mother. I'd done this teenager thing before.

So I understood.

We were at a delicate phase, Aaron and I, and I knew it. I didn't want to press, wanted him to reach out to me if he wanted to spend the evening in my presence. I'd known somewhere inside of me that I would be blown off. I wouldn't have gotten inebriated if I'd expected otherwise.

Disappointment sounded in my tone nonetheless when I finally replied. "Yes. The hotel."

The car signal clicked rhythmically as we waited at a light to turn uptown. I sunk back in my seat, letting myself remember, for a moment, the person I'd been when I'd wed. I'd felt so much older marrying a woman ten years my senior, but I was really such a child then, only twenty-five.

My, how I'd grown up since.

And now my thoughts turned back to Audrey, younger than I'd been when I'd married, but just as enthusiastic and charmed with love and life as I'd been.

I opened my texts and found where she'd sent herself a message.

AUDREY: A million people in the city, and you and I met. That's kismet.

I laughed out loud. My driver was spot on—she *was* fantastic. Fantastic and trusting and young and that was enough reason to delete both her number and the whimsical message from my phone.

But I saved it instead. Not because she'd hooked me, but because I needed to know it was her when she called. If she called.

She *wouldn't* call.

She couldn't have been more than ten years older than Aaron. Why would a girl her age have any interest in me? Our encounter had been one of the moment. It had been dark, and we were alone and tipsy and aroused by good conversation. Nothing else. It would be forgotten by tomorrow.

Though if she really could forget that kiss...

I was still thinking about the malleable way her lips fit to mine when I reached my hotel room on the Upper East Side. I'd forgotten and left the Do Not Disturb sign on my suite door when I'd left for the day so the bed was still rumpled and the pot for tea was still sitting on the desk. Sloppy and cluttered weren't usually my style. An embarrassing space to bring a woman back to, not that there was one with me now. Not that I'd thought about asking Audrey to accompany me to my room.

If I had, would she have said yes?

She may have, and I would have devoured her. Would have spent the whole night showing her all the ways a man could please a woman, ways that she yearned for but couldn't yet imagine.

Fantasizing about it made my earlier hard-on return. I took off my suit jacket and hung it on the back of the desk chair before I sat in it myself, fumbling with my belt, eager to play this daydream out with my cock in my hand.

But just as I got my zip down, I stopped, a sickening wave of guilt rolling over me. It felt crass and wrong to beat off to thoughts of this girl who could be my daughter. Even though she'd never know that I'd done it, it was degrading and a violation of sorts.

I zipped up my trousers and stood. I loosened my tie and then moved to the buttons of my shirt, undressing furiously. I needed a shower. A *cold* shower, that was what would take care of this.

Just as I dropped my shirt on the desk chair with my jacket, my mobile rang.

My heart leapt so high, it was practically in my throat as I scrambled to look at my screen, hoping it was *her* name that I'd see lighting up on the caller ID.

The name I saw instead caused me to let out a groan.

With resignation, I clicked the accept button and answered. "Hello, Ellen." Ellen Rachel Wallace Starkney Locke. She was just Ellen Wallace again now, having shed both the name I'd given her and the one she'd received in her previous marriage. Eight years had passed now since the paperwork had become final on our divorce, and still, she made my blood boil every time I had contact with her.

"I haven't even spoken yet, and you already have a tone," she greeted me, with a tone of her own. So nasty. So like Ellen.

Now there was a boner killer.

"Yes, I think I earned the right, don't you?" I didn't need to bring up her past sins against me. She knew them.

"Honestly, Dylan," she said, letting out an audible sigh. "Move on. I have. It's time you joined me."

I pinched the bridge of my nose. She was a liar. She hadn't moved on. She was still stuck underneath the emotional avalanche that had fallen upon her the day Amanda had died ten years ago. Instead of facing her pain, Ellen had buried it, becoming rotten and disconnected as she did.

If she'd really moved on, if she'd let herself heal, would she and I be apart today?

I couldn't imagine it. Didn't even want to anymore. Because I *had* moved on—moved on from her and any notion of happily ever after. She'd proven to me that love always died, and I'd accepted it. *She* was the one in denial.

I didn't want to go there with her, though, not tonight. "Why are you calling, Ellen? Anything you have to say could have been said to me tomorrow when I pick up Aaron."

"That's what I'm calling about. Aaron won't be able to see you until the afternoon. Oh, and then he has Latin lessons at four, so it will be evening, actually, before you can get him."

I ran my palm through my hair and clutched a handful tightly in frustration. "Christ, Ellen. He can't skip Latin one week while his father is in town? I flew from another continent to spend this time with him."

"Lessons are paid for in advance. There are no make-ups. Latin is a foundational language, and it's so important these days."

No. It wasn't. Not as important as spending time with his father.

But there was no rationalizing with the helicopter tiger mother that was Ellen Wallace. "And why is it I can't see him during the day? I chose this week to visit because he had time off from school."

"While he doesn't have school this week officially, to-morrow the teachers will be in the classrooms available for makeup work and tutoring. I signed Aaron up for the full day."

I leaned against the desk, my knuckles curled. Aaron didn't need tutoring or makeup. He had a three point four grade point average. This was Ellen being spiteful and stubborn.

"Cancel it. I can tutor him."

"On seventh-grade advanced chemistry?" she retorted patronizingly. "Even if you could understand it, he needs a lab."

"Why is a thirteen-year-old even taking advanced chemistry? Aaron doesn't have a scientific bone in his body. Are you shoving these classes down his throat?"

"I'm insuring his future," Ellen said, raising her voice.

"Ensuring that he's going to hate you one day, if not already. Cancel the tutoring."

"It's too late. He's signed up. And I'll not let you get in the way of his success."

"*His success*," I echoed incredulously. He was still just

a boy. Did she ever give him a chance to just be a kid? I was so angry, I went low. "I'll pick him up myself. I'll sign him out from the school as soon as you drop him off."

"It would be kidnapping. They won't let you take him without my authorization." She was just as nasty as I was. Nastier.

"I'm not on the school's parental records? We'd always agreed it would be both of us in case there was ever an emergency!"

"I reconsidered. If there was an emergency, you'd be too far away." She sounded proud of herself. "I have my sister listed as emergency now. And Donovan Kincaid is there as a backup to her."

I had to stop myself from kicking the chair, and only because I was concerned that I'd break a toe with as hard as I wanted to kick it. "Donovan Kincaid doesn't know what to do with a kid. This is you trying to keep him from me, like you always do." This conversation reaffirmed my decision to get a second apartment in New York City— so that I could visit more often and have more access to Aaron.

"I'm not keeping him from anyone. You are delusional."

"And you're ice. Cold and bitter and mean. Exactly the qualities that drove me to leave you." Maybe I was going there after all.

"You didn't leave me because I was cold and bitter. You left because I cheated on you." She'd destroyed my heart with her betrayal and she almost sounded like she was gloating.

To hell with her.

"You were ice cold and bitter before that. It simply

took the act of you cheating on me to recognize that I couldn't..." I paused and inhaled deeply. I didn't need to relive this. I didn't want to remember how deeply I'd once believed in her. In us.

"That you couldn't save me?" she finished for me. "Couldn't make me whole again? Is that what you were going to say?" She was callous and cruel as she pointed out how naïve I had been to think that I could love her better.

Yes, Ellen, we are in agreement there.

I'd been stupid in those romantic notions. I was wiser now. And I didn't see any point in returning to naivety, regardless of the pull my heart occasionally gave.

"I'm picking Aaron up from school when he's done with the day," I said firmly, refusing to dwell on the past any longer. "I'll make sure he reviews his Latin before I drop him off at home. And, by God, Ellen, you better have me approved to retrieve him or I'll get my solicitor involved." Then, before she could refute me, I said good night and clicked off the phone.

What a goddamned shrew.

I was energized with rage, my heart racing with the power of it.

But underneath my temper was a dangerous longing. A yearning for a different time. A time when I could afford the innocent enthusiasm for human connection. Before I knew how cruel people could be. Before I understood the downfalls of being vulnerable.

What a rose-colored world it had been—a prettier, more tolerable world—when I'd believed wholeheartedly in commitments and forever. When lust and love were two sides of the same coin. Sex, an expression of feelings rather than just a pleasurable release.

I longed to be free of the reality that I wore like chains around my neck.

And then! Then I could ask a girl back to my hotel room without caring about age differences or impropriety or what state my suite had been left in. I could get lost in the breathlessness of her kiss, not worrying about anyone's feelings or what might inevitably happen if I put my trust in her embrace. I could imagine it so vividly, what it would be like to be that kind of a man again, what it would be like to kiss a girl like Audrey, undress her, teach her. Make love to her.

My trousers were bulging again with the fantasy. I was throbbing and thick. I couldn't make it to the shower if I tried.

I shoved down my trousers and pulled out my cock, fisting it with my right hand as I sat down on the chair. With my eyes closed, I remembered vividly the weight of Audrey on my lap, remembered the pleasurable burn of her rubbing up and down along the imprisoned length of my hard-on. Remembered the press of her breasts against my chest, her nipples so taut they spiked through the layers of clothing between us. Remembered her mouth as it gave in to my wicked desire, my tongue caressing and schooling her at once. My lips memorizing her and debauching her.

My palm stroked angrily across the inflamed skin of my cock, faster and faster, punishing myself even as the pleasure built and built and built, like static on a balloon when rubbed against a headful of hair. Like stockinged feet, trudged across the carpet. Like too many plugs jammed into a wall socket, my orgasm surged through me with electrical shock. Cum spilled out over my fist as I tugged and tugged, past the point of comfort, until everything inside me had fallen in thick ropes across my bare stomach, dirty and filthy and obscene.

I sat for several minutes, staring at the mess I'd made, my hands shaking from the release as, little by little, the delirious flash of bliss dissolved into cold, hard reality.

I was alone. I would always be alone.

I'd learned the hard way that alone was the most sensible way to live.

There was no benefit of vulnerability. There was no "making love." There was no reason to trust. Hearts were for pumping oxygen through the body. They didn't break. They beat on.

Audrey had called me a liar when she'd suggested that I secretly believed in her religion of romance, but she was wrong.

I wasn't a liar. I was a man who could no longer believe in the lie.

CHAPTER FOUR

Audrey

"H e *kissed* you?"

Of course I told my sister.

I told her as soon as she walked through the door. Mostly, because I wanted to be sure it wouldn't be a surprise if Dylan said anything to her, but also because I shared everything with Sabrina.

Well, almost everything. I never actually talked about sex with her, but that was because she had a barrier like a thirteen inch cement wall surrounding her when it came to the subject. Talking about sex made her tense and agitated. I'd decided that meant she was either asexual or into some weird stuff in the bedroom. Not that I'd knock her either way.

"More like *I* kissed *him*," I said, since I'd initiated the whole thing. I didn't want her to get the wrong idea about the situation. Because there had been absolutely nothing wrong about that kiss at all—except that it had been too short.

Just remembering the way Dylan's mouth fit so perfectly against mine brought a swarm of butterflies to my tummy.

"You *kissed* my boss?" Sabrina seemed to be having a hard time wrapping her head around the fact. Obviously she was stuck on her own relationship with the man.

But I'd already thought about that.

I kicked off my shoes and pulled my knees underneath me on the couch. "Dylan is not actually your boss. He's more like your boss's equal, if you want to be technical." And, to be fair, she herself was sleeping with a different man who was her boss's equal. If there wasn't an issue there, why would there be an issue with me?

She dropped her coat and purse on the back of the sofa and put a stern fist on her hip—one of the postures she took when she was assuming a motherly role with me. "If you want to be technical, he's old enough to be your father."

I rolled my eyes. "He is not. He's just experienced and wise." To be honest, I wasn't actually sure of Dylan's age.

"He's twenty years older than you."

Huh. I'd guessed more like fifteen. "Maybe I have a thing for dads." I didn't, I didn't think, but I *could*. Could I? Was that the comfort I'd been unable to replicate with my previous boyfriends? "Don't knock my kink. I don't knock yours." I was possibly more defensive than I needed to be.

Sabrina's jaw slammed shut, and she got that tense, agitated way she did when sex conversations turned a spotlight on her.

So then she was definitely into some weird bedroom stuff. Interesting.

Finally, she sighed. "Fine. I won't knock the age difference." She came around to the front of the couch and sank down next to me. "I don't actually care what you're into anyway, as long as it's consensual. I just don't want you getting hurt. Dylan doesn't seem into relationships. You get that, right? Not to mention that you live on entirely different continents."

I had been defensive before, but now I was incensed. "It was just a kiss! God. I'm not planning to marry the guy." I stretched my legs out in front of me and studied my toes so I didn't have to look at her. She was being dramatic.

Even though it *hadn't* been just a kiss.

It had been the *best* kiss. It had been grinding and thrusting and heavy petting. It had told me everything I needed to know about Dylan—that he was skilled and sensitive and seduceable. It had been the stars aligning, bringing a man who needed to be reminded to let his emotions loose together with me, a woman who needed practice getting physically loose.

But Sabrina was skeptical. "Just a kiss," she repeated.

Did I mention she was being dramatic? Just because I'd fallen hard and fast for a few men that didn't work out didn't mean that I didn't know how to protect myself. It didn't mean that I wanted to change who I was, either. I was a girl who felt things. I knew who I was. I knew what I was made of—big emotions packed into a little body. And keeping all those feelings pent up in such a small space was impossible. I couldn't stuff my passion into some dark corner of my soul the way Sabrina did. I lived from the heart. I loved with my entirety. I loved frequently and deeply, and if that meant I hurt sometimes—or a lot of times—so be it. My heartbreaks shaped me into who I was.

And I *liked* who I was.

All that being said, love wasn't the reason I was drawn to Dylan. He was an opportunity that I couldn't pass up, a choice I almost couldn't help but make. Opportunity knocked, but Fate had seemed to be at the door as well.

Seeing how the conversation had gone so far, though, I really didn't think Sabrina was in a place to understand the whole truth.

I settled for partial honesty, peering up at her with a sigh. "I felt bad for the guy. All that doom and gloom. 'Love's dead. Grump, grump.' He needed something nice for a change."

She narrowed her gaze. "So you thought you'd kiss him and that would show him. Make him magically believe in hearts and romance again?"

"Shut up." Now she was just being mean. Would she always think of me as the little girl she had to parent? She wasn't my mother. And little girls grew up eventually.

I slumped in my seat and pouted. "You think I'm naïve."

She gave me a look that said she very much wanted to lecture me, but when she leaned toward me, it was just to kiss me on the head. "I think you're amazing," she said.

And I grinned at her. Not because she'd told me I was amazing—she was my sister; she was sort of obligated to think that—but because *she* was amazing. She'd basically been my mother since she was thirteen years old. I knew it took an effort for her to let me make my own choices, make my own mistakes. I was proud of her for fighting against her instincts.

Maybe her latest relationship was changing her for the good.

Which reminded me, she and I had parted this evening

when she'd left with her "boyfriend," and all we'd talked about since she'd gotten home was me.

I wasn't amazing, after all.

I nudged her with my shoulder. "Hey. Tell me what happened with Donovan."

We spent the next half an hour talking about her night and *her* kiss—seems I hadn't been the only Lind girl to get some action from a Reach CEO. Then, after I'd convinced her to look on the bright side about her romantic situation, I said good night and slipped into her guest room.

It wasn't even ten o'clock, still early, considering that I was used to staying up until two in the morning most nights with my graduate studies, but Sabrina had to work in the morning, and I didn't want to be the reason she was dragging her feet come six a.m.

I was hardly tired, though. The buzz from the dinner's wine had long ago worn off, and there was a new energy stirring in me. An excited energy. An energy that had me fidgeting and restless in the queen bed I had all to myself.

The excitement was over Dylan and the freaking insane way he knew how to use his mouth. I could imagine those lips elsewhere on my body—along the curve of my jaw, down my neck. Lower, lower. Lower still.

I'd had men go down on me, but I'd never had one give me an orgasm. I bet Dylan knew how to satisfy a woman that way. I could tell by how he controlled our kiss with his tongue. He was more alpha than he appeared, with his brooding British act. It was refreshing, considering how many guys I'd been with who had been all around nice guys, including under the covers. Too nice. So nice they didn't know when to add a little pressure or another finger or even a hair tug.

Dylan was polite, but he wasn't nice. He was respectful, but he was also aggressive. He'd practically had me coming just from our makeout session, and he hadn't even gotten his fingers inside my panties.

If that was what an older man could do, I was never planning to date a guy my age again.

I turned on my sexiest Spotify list and replayed the memory, letting the heat and electricity rush through my body like it had when I had been with Dylan. My panties were damp again. The space between my thighs ached, and if I weren't in a bed that didn't belong to me, I would have put my hand down and rubbed the desire away.

Instead, I just held the feeling, held the buzz, let it gather within me until every part of my skin was humming and alive. It made for a restless sleep when I shut the lights out hours later, after I'd taken a shower and sketched a bit in my notepad.

It would be worth it, though, I was sure of it. And it wouldn't be long until I got relief, if everything went the way I hoped it would.

I waited until Sabrina had left before coming out of my room for breakfast. I didn't want her to drill me about my plans for the day, and boy, did I have plans.

First, I hustled over to a boutique lingerie shop nearby Sabrina's Midtown apartment. They were on holiday schedule and opened early, so I got what I needed and was at the register well before ten.

With my purchases "in hand," so to say, I finally pulled out my phone to get ahold of Dylan. Sure, I could have texted him before I'd gone shopping, but I didn't want to seem desperate, contacting him before the sun had reached a decent place in the sky. Because I wasn't desperate. I was *eager*. There was a difference, I was sure.

I had, however, composed my text the night before so it was ready to go with just a press of the send button.

AUDREY: Happy Tuesday! Did U sleep OK?

Polite, harmless. A message that wouldn't scare him off.

Still, he took his time answering. Almost seven whole minutes. Thankfully there was a Starbucks next door so I had a Venti chai tea and a place to sit by the time he responded.

DYLAN: I slept well, thank you for asking. And you?

I giggled softly at his formality.

AUDREY: Well enough.

If tossing and turning to a night full of erotic dreams was considered well, anyway.

AUDREY: What are ur plans for today?

DYLAN: I have an appointment with an estate agent to look at an apartment.

I practically squealed. He'd mentioned at dinner that he was looking to buy a place in the city so he could visit his son more often, a place he could eventually give to his son, if he wanted it. But I hadn't realized he would actually be looking today.

> AUDREY: Oh, goody! I'll join u. Tell
> me where?

While he'd taken his time responding to each of my texts so far, this one came in almost immediately.

> DYLAN: Ah, no. I don't think that's
> a good idea.

I wasn't at all discouraged. I was expecting his hesitation. He was a proper man, after all, and oftentimes the things that happened in the dark seemed less than proper in the light of day.

> AUDREY: It's an excellent idea! U
> can't get a place w/out a 2nd opinion
> & I have very good taste.

> DYLAN: I'm sure you do, but I have
> this handled.

I sipped from my tea, considering what tactic to take next.

> AUDREY: Come on. Rn't U curious about
> the kismet?

> DYLAN: Still playing that game, are
> you?

He hadn't said no, which meant he *was* curious. How could he not be? I'd felt his *curiosity* poking at me last night while I straddled his lap.

This text had also come in right away. Which meant I

was right about my assessment of Dylan Locke so far—the man responded well to taunting.

I could do taunting. I could do it very well.

AUDREY: Find out.

Two little words. They'd do the trick.

Bingo.

Less than a minute later I had an address and a time to meet him. I knew I had taunting down. It was in other areas that I lacked expertise.

For the time being, anyway.

CHAPTER FIVE

Dylan

I thought she'd be less dangerous in the sunlight.

I was wrong.

She walked into the lobby of the apartment building in Sutton Place, dressed in a red flowy thing that stopped mid-calf and a stylish coat that hit mid-thigh. Her tawny brown hair was loose around her shoulders. But the piece de resistance was the high-heeled black boots that disappeared under her hem. After fantasizing about her the night before, it was impossible not to imagine those shoes wrapped around my waist—wrapped around my face—her body naked and trembling. She was sex on heels, and I was a goner.

But lust wasn't the only reason I found myself fascinated with her. She and I had shared an evening together, shared the same space, shared the same air, and yet the life that oxygen breathed into her was much different than the life breathed into mine. She inflated into someone animated and vivacious while I was left hollow and shriveled and wrinkled—metaphorically if not exactly literally. It intrigued me. It was like the old adage about onlookers unable to look away from a train wreck, only I was the train wreck, and I couldn't stop looking when something so unblemished and uncorrupted walked past.

I'd been like her once, hardened by the lessons of reality over the years. While I felt surely she'd have her own dose of truth in time, the thought made me grim. Couldn't she be spared from the spoils of heartache? If I were a praying man, or even a man who wished for impossible things, I may have spent a great deal of time asking for just that. For Audrey Lind to leave this world as is, unscathed. Unbitter.

Still a believer.

"It's a fantastic part of the city!" Audrey exclaimed, skipping a greeting while I remained transfixed on the bubblegum pink of her lips. "I've never been to the Upper East Side. It has so much more charm than I'd expected."

"Yes, well, I wanted to be within walking distance of both Aaron's home and school." I hadn't thought particularly much about the borough except that it suited Ellen— snooty and elitist. I'd focused so much on that angle that I'd forgotten there were charms to the city that were untainted by my ex.

Audrey began an earnest inspection of the building, circling around me to take everything in. "First impressions are good. The lobby is clean, well-furnished. Both a doorman and a security desk—that's a nice touch." She frowned suddenly. "It's strange that they have a reprint of John Constable as the major focal point."

I tilted my head at the hanging art. I hadn't noticed the familiar piece before she pointed it out, and I wouldn't have remembered the artist's name without her mention of it. The original was hanging in the National Gallery, if I remembered correctly. It depicted a man with his hay cart and horses in the River between Essex and Suffolk counties. There was a peace and beauty in the image that I couldn't put into words.

"You don't like it?" I was surprised at her indignation at such an unsuspecting painting.

She turned her frown on me. "John Constable? I love his work. He's quite a snob about your homeland, but he showed that landscape images are not just beautiful but also powerful. I'm just curious why a luxury building would choose a cheap recreation of a famous art piece—albeit in a rather hefty frame—rather than purchasing something unique and original by a local artist. It would definitely class up the place, and it seems that is what they're going for. Maybe I should give the suggestion to the doorman." She'd already taken two steps toward the door before she finished talking.

Who did that? Who had thoughts on everything—lovely thoughts and bold thoughts, on art and luxury apartment buildings—and then proceeded to share them with no inhibitions?

Who was this woman?

And what was she doing in my life?

"Audrey, why are you here?"

My question halted her task. She spun around in my direction. "Hmm?"

"Why are you here?" A simple but pressing question.

Slowly, with a subtle grin, she strode toward me, her heels clicking on the marble floor. "You invited me. Don't you remember?"

"I'm pretty sure that's not how that went." My eyes searched aimlessly over my shoes as I attempted to recall how we ended up there together. It all happened so quickly, my hands responding to her texts without giving my brain a chance to weigh in. "No, you lured me."

"I *lured* you? How is that possible when I'm the one who has joined *you* on your day's plans? It seems, Dylan Locke, that you may have lured *me*."

Her expression was so convincing, I momentarily doubted myself. "No, no. I most definitely didn't lure you. You lured me with your talk of fate and finding out what it had to do with us."

"Kismet," she corrected.

"Yes, that's right. *Kismet*. You dangled the word out in front of me the way a fisherman dangles a—"

"Hook?" she guessed.

I narrowed my eyes. "*Lure*."

Her smile widened. "That's amazing that a simple text message could hold that much power over you. Why do you think that is, do you suppose?"

And that was the real question, more important than why she was here. The question about why I was tempting myself with something I was never going to believe in. About why her particular lure was so irresistible. The question I'd hoped she'd be able to answer because I was at a loss.

A question that wasn't getting answered now either because the estate agent I had an appointment with was currently walking toward me with his hand stretched out.

"Mr. Locke? Jeff Jones, nice to meet you." He finished his handshake with one hand and immediately his other passed over a business card, which I immediately pocketed without looking at. I knew everything I needed to about the man from our encounter thus far. He was a salesman, a charmer. Trendy with his trimmed beard and fitted suit. Good-looking, perhaps, but if I'd had my guess, he'd had work done. His jaw was too square. His nose too straight.

All that mattered was that he had the ability to put in a competitive offer, and the ambitious air surrounding him suggested he could.

"Sorry I'm running a tad bit late," he went on, talking in that fast New York style I still hadn't become accustomed to even after the years I'd lived here. "I had a closing this morning that ran long. There are no showings on the books today for this unit, though, so we'll have plenty of time to spend in the apartment."

His focus turned to Audrey then, and his voice suddenly shifted in tone. "Well, hello there…?"

"Audrey," she said, offering her hand in greeting.

"It's a pleasure, Audrey." The smarmy way Jeff Jones held Audrey's hand, said her name, and stared too long made me want to sock him in his too perfect nose. He was too old to be flirting with her. Jeff Jones had to be at least…

At least my age.

That realization was a punch, all right. In my gut.

And that was just a warm-up to the next blow. "Mr. Locke, I didn't know you'd be bringing your daughter. Glad to have you both here."

I felt my jaw drop and then lock up, frozen in horror.

At the same time, my cock stirred.

Audrey, fortunately, remained composed. Draping her arm over my shoulder, her eyes twinkled mischievously.

"He wanted my opinion, didn't you Daddy? We're very close."

Very funny, my scowl said. I considered correcting her until it dawned on me the situation looked better this way. As long as no one noticed the bulging of my trousers every time she addressed me with the parental term, anyway.

Shopping for a flat with a girl half my age...what was I thinking?

Perhaps she wasn't as young as I gave her credit for.

The estate agent excused himself to grab the key from the lockbox at the security desk. As soon as he was out of earshot, I asked quietly, "How young are you exactly?"

Audrey batted her lashes in my direction. "Are you asking how old I am? I'm twenty-three."

I nearly choked.

Nineteen years between us.

I'd lost my virginity later than I'd wanted, at the age of seventeen. If I'd knocked that woman up, our child would still be older than Audrey Lind.

It was mortifying.

The realization didn't make me want to kiss her any less. It just gave me a sufficient amount of guilt about the desire to make kissing her again seem totally worth it.

I was still stewing about the years between us when Jeff returned and led us into the lift. He pushed the button for the thirty-second floor, chattering on about the building amenities and the maintenance upkeep.

I was barely listening.

"Are you okay?" Audrey whispered.

"Just thinking about how old I feel next to you." That

wasn't exactly true. I was lamenting the difference in our ages, but she didn't make me feel old. She made me feel quite young. Younger than I deserved to feel. Her youth was contagious.

"Do you want to know how I feel next to you?" She linked her arm around mine. "Bold."

Bold. Jesus. I felt like I needed to loosen my tie, except I wasn't wearing one.

The lift opened on our floor, and Jeff Jones started out the door and down the hall, not paying much attention to us as we followed. Thank God. Since I still had Audrey's hand on my bicep. Her palm felt warm even through my jumper and the button-up underneath. Like a hot iron. Like a brand from the devil reminding me she might look like an angel but she'd been sent from hell.

Gently, I shrugged her off and doubled my steps to catch up to our estate agent.

My estate agent. There was no *our* here.

Jeff continued promoting the apartment's highlights as he unlocked the door and stood aside for us to enter. Instantly, I was pleased—both with the condition of the unit and the opportunity to concentrate on something other than the young woman attempting to rock my world. I was familiar with the layout of the two-bedrooms in this particular building. An acquaintance from my New York days had lived here, and wanting to purchase the same for myself, I'd diligently watched the realty notices from London until something came up. It was small in comparison to my flat in England, but exactly what I had in mind. Clean, simple. Well laid out. On property, there was a gym, a pool, billiards tables, a large courtyard. A gem in the city and for a decent price.

I opened the foyer cupboard and found it empty, save for a few stray hangers. Before I could close it again, Audrey was there, peering inside.

"Nice, sturdy bar," she said, tugging on the garment rod. She unbuttoned her coat and peeled it off.

Jeff Jones, gentleman that he was, immediately appeared at her side to hang it up.

I stood dumbstruck, seeing for the first time the entirety of Audrey's outfit. She was wearing a wrap dress. A sexy, fitted thing with only a tie separating her underclothing from the eyes of the world. *Kill me now.*

I had to turn away.

Pretending she wasn't there, I made my way through the rest of the apartment ahead of her, checking out the bathroom and the second bedroom before making my way to the main living area. The space was staged and styled with traditional furniture in fashionable colors, a look that I made a note to mimic after I purchased, with one addition—curtains. It was a corner unit, and the large windows surrounding the room delivered views of both the river and the city. Stunning as they were, the lack of window coverings meant no privacy. People in the building across the street could look right in if they had a mind to.

"Incredible!" Audrey gasped from behind me. She ran giddily to look outside, stopping several feet short of the actual windows.

"You don't feel the true impact without getting close up." I'd apparently forgotten my determination to pretend she wasn't there.

"That's okay. I'm good right here. I'm afraid of heights." She glanced quickly to Jeff Jones who'd entered the room with her. "You know that, Daddy," she added, remembering her ruse.

I hadn't thought she could be afraid of anything, daring and impetuous that she was. This new insight added to the enigma of Audrey Lind. Part wildling, part devil, part innocent, all contradiction.

"I thought you'd grown out of it," I muttered. Whatever was I doing, playing along?

And she was invading my space again, standing too close, smelling too good. Making my jumper feel too hot and my throat feel too tight.

I had to hurry this tour up.

Sticking my hands in my trouser pockets, I turned to the agent. "The website said this unit is up for lease as well as for sale. Rentals are allowed in the HOA amendments, then?"

Jones perked at the potential sale. "Yes. Is that of interest to you?"

"I'm not planning to be here year-round, so yes. I may consider leasing it out." Frankly, I was just as happy to leave it empty, a safe space for Aaron to hide out as he got older. Ellen would surely disapprove, which was half the appeal. "There's no one living here now?"

"Not at this moment. But!" He was winding up for his big pitch. I could feel it. "This unit has had several showings just in the last few days."

Not likely with the weather and the approaching holiday.

"If it gets rented out before an offer comes in, the lease will have to be dealt with in negotiations. It's another reason to act fast if you're serious about buying."

I'd have an offer in before the day was over, though

I wasn't ready to admit it. But, even if I paid cash and rushed a closing, I wouldn't be in the unit before I left New York this time at the end of the week.

The idea of being in there sooner, to have the breathing room and get away from the stuffiness of the hotel, suddenly appealed to me. "I could, you're telling me, put in an offer and also apply for a lease at the same time."

"That's correct. If you want to try it out and see how it works before you decide to purchase, or if you want to move in right away, that's exactly what I'd recommend. You could be in here as soon as tomorrow, in fact."

Audrey edged up beside me, the heat of her a pleasant nuisance.

I felt my muscles tighten as I fought to remain focused. "It comes furnished?"

"Yes."

"I'd like to fill out a rental application." It was still early in the day. I'd push to be in by that evening.

"Sure, sure! I didn't realize you'd be interested in renting as well, so I didn't bring the application, but we can get that all settled if you just come with me to the leasing office. It's only a few blocks away. No more than a fifteen minute walk. Or if you'd rather grab a cab, it'll take just about as long."

I wouldn't rather grab a cab. And I wasn't interested in walking fifteen minutes in the snow and slush. I was irritated at the man's lack of foresight. Wasn't there an application at the desk along with the lockbox? What a professional faux pas.

The agent didn't seem to register my annoyance.

Audrey, on the other hand, read me completely.

"Mr. Jones," she said, her tone pure honey. "Jeff." She left my side to cozy up against the salesman, immediately triggering a rush of envy through my veins. I might have stopped her, even, if I weren't so curious about her motives.

"It's so cold outside today," she went on, swirling the tip of her finger in a giant O on the shoulder of Jones' suit jacket. "I've just started getting warm. You wouldn't mind terribly going and getting the application and bringing it back for us, would you? I know Daddy would love to have the extra time looking around the place."

Her coy manipulation, the sweet pout of her mouth, the damn use of the word *daddy*—I wouldn't be able to walk to the lift at this point, let alone to an office three blocks away.

I was a sick fuck. There was no doubt about it.

Jones hemmed and hawed. "Oh. I don't know about that. I'm really not supposed to leave you alone here."

He hadn't moved away from the girl, though. His dilated eyes and flushed face said he was under her spell and loving it. In front of her father, no less!

Fake father. But he didn't know that.

"Oh, but, Jeff!" Audrey batted her eyelashes. "He's going to buy it! Or, he will if he has the proper time to decide. There's a pretty significant commission on this unit, isn't there? I'd hate for you to lose out simply because of a silly, little rule."

She was good. So very good.

"Your daughter is sure convincing." Jones smiled nervously in my direction, appearing to be equally taken with her abilities. "Okay. All right. I'm sure it will be fine. I'll be back in about thirty minutes then?" He was headed to the exit, as though determined to be back as soon as possible.

At the foyer, he paused to look from me to Audrey with an anxious plea in his eyes. "Please don't do, well, don't... hurt...anything." I heard him muttering on to himself as the door shut behind him. Something that sounded a lot like *I better not regret this.*

Which left me with my own regrets, namely the seductress in my midst.

"That was quite impressive," I said, not quite sure if I should have gone with the man rather than be left alone with her. Alone. So near a bed. And other furniture that could be used for fornication.

She winked. "I have my talents."

Yes, she did. I was learning how skilled she was at wrapping men twice her age around her little pinkie. And now I was quite sure I should have left when I'd had the chance.

Still, she had me on that string, towing me toward her when I should be swimming away. Could I even swim away at this point? Understanding how my fate was tied up in her—never mind that it was because she masterminded the whole thing—I considered giving in to the pull.

I circled her, studying every delicious curve. "The thing I don't understand as of yet is why it was so important to you that he let us stay here?"

I stopped when I was facing her again so I had the full vantage point when she undid the tie at the side of her dress, shrugged it off her shoulders, and let it drop to the floor.

Audrey Lind in nothing but her high-heeled boots and the naughtiest pair of matching panties and bra I'd ever seen on a woman.

Goddamn, this apartment really needed curtains.

CHAPTER SIX

Audrey

Dylan seemed to go pale. He normally had rather fair skin—probably because he was British and because his work habits didn't let him out in the sun too often—but now he was even whiter than usual.

Maybe it was a bit scandalous to just drop my dress the way I had. I could have talked to him about my plan first, but after the way he'd kissed me the night before, I didn't think conversation was necessary. I was certainly still buzzing from the feel of his lips and the sweep of his tongue. I thought a little skin would be all that was needed to reignite those passions in him as well.

Instead, it seemed to throw him into a state of shock.

"Audrey," he stammered, his eyes darting everywhere, then to me, then quickly to anywhere else but me. He was deliberately trying not to look, but it seemed he couldn't help himself. "What the bloody hell are you doing, girl?" He picked my dress up off the floor and brought it to me. "Put this on. Please. There aren't curtains. The whole city can see you!"

I glanced behind him at the windows. We were too high for anyone to see in through the street, and the apartments across the way didn't have the floor-to-ceiling glass that this unit had. It was unlikely anyone could see me from there either.

I took the dress from him anyway. Then tossed it over my shoulder to the ground. "I don't care if everyone can see me. I only care if you see me."

This made the color return to his face.

"And as for what I'm doing," I continued, stepping toward him, but before I could say more he interrupted.

"If you have more to say then could you please do it from the couch? Which is over there. A safe distance from me."

He muttered the last part so quietly that I wasn't even sure I was supposed to hear it.

It made me smile. He really was quite adorable. "If it makes you more comfortable." I shrugged.

"It does."

"Well, then." I didn't mind humoring him. And torturing him simultaneously. I sat on the sofa, crossing one leg over the other, hoping the slow, seductive routine didn't come off as clumsy and embarrassing. Just because I felt confident didn't mean I knew what I was doing. Hence this entire kismet project.

Dylan immediately lined himself up between me and the window, using his body to make up for the lack of blinds.

See? Adorable.

"As you were saying," he prompted.

"As I was saying." I took a breath in and let it out. "Here's the deal—I've had two serious boyfriends in my life. Two men that I've had sex with, and I didn't sleep with either of them until we'd said the L word. Which is to say, I don't do this. Ever."

"Mm hmm." His arms were crossed over his chest and he nodded furiously, as though urging me to go on.

So I did. "With both of them the sex was blah."

"Right. You didn't find either of them compatible. Yes, yes. You told me this last night. I remember. How exactly does this lead to you standing naked in my flat?"

"Not your flat yet, Dylan," I teased. "And not naked. I have lingerie on. Purchased just for you." I uncrossed my legs, stretched them out in front of me, and leaned back on my palms so he could have the best view of my ensemble. "Do you like?"

"I, uh." He cleared his throat. "I do like. Very much."

The piercing gaze he hit me with made my heart trip and my skin prickle with goosebumps.

"But that doesn't explain the, um…" He gestured toward me with his entire hand. "This."

I chuckled. "I'm getting there. I was getting there last night, too, just, your lips became a distraction." Maybe I'd gone over the top in the flirtation department, but it didn't make the statement any less true. Besides, it was worth it to see the color in his cheeks deepen and the crotch of his pants expand while he let himself remember our kiss.

It was especially worth it because of how *much* his pants expanded. Dang, that man was hung.

After a distracted beat, I went on. "Anyway. After my last breakup, I decided that I needed to get the sex ed out of the way before I settle down. So. Isn't it kismet that I met you? An experienced man who is only interested in banging? Wouldn't you like to bang me now? Show me how it's done?"

He inhaled sharply then clutched his chest with one hand, wiping at his forehead with the other as he fell back against the glass behind him.

I stood up, panicked. "Dylan! Are you okay? Are you having a heart attack?" I rushed to him, but he waved me away and stumbled toward the couch.

"I'm fine, I'm fine. As long as you stay there, several feet from me, I'm fine."

Not his heart, then, but a good old-fashioned panic attack.

I gave him a lazy grin. "How many feet away? Like is this too close?" I stepped predatorily near him. "Or how about this?" Another step.

"It's all too close. All of it. You and me in this same flat is too close." He circled around the sofa, backing away from me as though I were a demon about to put a hex on him.

"Why ever would you say that?" I asked innocently, following every step he took. "If anything, I'd say we aren't close enough."

"No, no, no. This is not appropriate. This shouldn't be happening. You should have your clothes on, for God's sake. I shouldn't have even allowed you to come here."

His rant felt directed more to himself than to me, but I continued to engage. "That's a terrible thing to say! Aren't we having fun together? The whole 'daddy' game with your realtor? That was a good time, wasn't it?"

He laughed incredulously as he rounded back to the front of the couch, one arm held out before himself as if to ward me off. "A good time is not the term I'd... Okay, yes, it was a fun bluff, but... Your sister is an employee in my firm! You are twenty years my junior!"

"Is it really twenty?" I'd told him my age, but he hadn't mentioned his to me. Sabrina hadn't even been certain. Not that it mattered. The important thing was that we were attracted to each other. That we had chemistry. And we definitely had that, whether he wanted to admit it or not.

"Yes, I'm sure. Or, it's nearly twenty. Nineteen, to be precise."

"Nineteen." I thought about that for a minute, growing more comfortable with the idea by the moment. "That's kind of hot, isn't it? That a woman that you're interested in who is nineteen years your junior is throwing herself at you? Begging you to teach her a thing or two. Or seven."

I'd closed in on him while I was talking, trapping him against the armchair. He didn't realize until he'd tripped and fell backward into the seat, but he'd only caught the edge in his fall and immediately slipped to the ground.

And I slipped right into his lap.

I spread my legs, straddling him the way I had the night before. His breath came fast, but even, and his skin was hot to the touch as I swept my finger across his forehead, brushing away the hair that had fallen there. He locked his eyes on mine, the pupils darkening as they lingered in his stare.

"I'm supposing you don't need CPR," I teased. I was terrible, but he was too easy.

His gaze narrowed. "My heart is fine. It's my morals that I'm struggling with."

"Because I'm so young? Because of Sabrina?"

"Yes. Even if we can ignore that I'm your sister's superior I am definitely old enough to be..." He shook his head, unable to finish the sentence.

"My father? I told you I thought that was hot. Are you going to tell me it doesn't interest you at all?"

He didn't answer but swallowed, his Adam's apple bobbing with the action.

"Because I won't believe you if you do. There's definitive proof to the contrary."

He scowled even as I could feel his body relaxing underneath me. "What proof?"

"This bad boy." I ground my hips, rubbing against his erection, nearly moaning from the thickness of it.

"There's a near-naked beautiful woman sitting on him. He can't help himself. He has a mind of his own and is not always in agreement with my decisions." Contrary to his words, he stroked a single finger up my arm, sending a shiver down my spine.

Even this...even just the deliberate way he touched me was more experienced than the men I'd been with. Boys, really, fumbling to get their cock inside me without any sort of prelude. My dirty professor was a *man*. Someone who knew exactly what to do with a woman. Who could show me how to handle him in return.

"He perked up long before I was sitting on him," I said, tilting my hips again.

This time he was the one to shudder. "You noticed that then?"

"It was quite hard to miss."

His lips turned up into a cocky smile as he drew his

finger further up my arm, over my shoulder to the strap of my bra. He fiddled with the thin elastic, so leisurely, so carefully, that I thought I might explode when he finally touched me for real.

Once more, I tilted my hips back and then forward, tracing the stiff length of his cock with the damp crotch panel of my panties. I'd meant it to hurry him up, urge him into kissing me, but it felt so good that I was the one who threw my head back and sighed.

Next thing I knew, I was on my back, on the floor, my hands pinned above my head with Dylan stretched out above me.

Wow. That move was...wow. So manly and take-charge-like. So alpha and swoony.

Somehow, he was even more good-looking from this angle. His expression was serious and heated, the creases near his eyes intense as he focused on me.

My heart thumped against my rib cage, pounding, pounding at the possibility of what was to come next.

"You don't seem to need any lessons in the art of se-duction," he said sternly. Fatherly, almost, except for the sexy, rough edge to his voice.

"You're right. I know how to seduce a man." I spread my legs, making room for him to settle in between my thighs. His eyes closed briefly as the ridge of his erection sunk down across my center. "What I don't know is how to tell a man what I like. How can I if I don't know what I like myself? If no one has ever shown me anything worth repeating."

He studied me silently for a moment. Every second felt like thirty as I measured time with the rapid lift and fall of my chest, waiting for him to make the next move, waiting for him to agree.

"And you think I can show you what you might like?" His gaze shifted to my mouth then back to my eyes.

I licked my lips in anticipation of the kiss he was obviously looking forward to as much as I was. "You've already shown me more than you can know."

His expression said he doubted that. "Assuming that's true...how do I know you won't fall for me in the process? You don't have a track record to prove you can separate sex from love."

Wasn't that a killer of a question?

He had every right to ask. I wasn't the least bit upset about it, though it did make me feel like the wind had been sucked out of my chest. Made me feel dizzy and unsure when just a moment ago I'd been drowning in confidence.

"I guess..." I started out tentatively, formulating the answer as I gave it. "I guess you *don't* know that. I guess I don't really know it either. I could try to convince you it isn't your problem—I'll be gone at the end of the week, and you'll be on the other side of the ocean—but I have a feeling you're the kind of guy that would very much think it was his problem, no matter where he was. You might not be fond of the love emotion, but you do recognize it in other people. That you acknowledge the weight it can carry might be what makes me feel so safe with you."

That was a revelation. I hadn't quite realized why I trusted him to be the guy to take on this task. We'd only just met. I shouldn't be this sure about him. But, just like he was afraid of how I'd react to this arrangement because I'd shown enough of myself for him to know it was a possibility, I also had seen enough of him to know I trusted him.

"I trust you," I told him. "I trust you to be careful with my body, and I trust that you won't lead me on in any way. That's a good start, isn't it?"

Before he could say anything, I pushed forward, my words tumbling out rapidly. "And what I can tell you for sure is that I don't have any *intentions* of becoming emotionally wrapped up in you. I *am* attracted to you. Crazy attracted to you. Turn-my-insides-into-mush kind of attracted to you, but I've always been able to separate attraction from real feelings. I've been crazy attracted to men before, given a few blow jobs to some of them, even, but I've only fallen in hard love with those two guys. Guys I *hadn't* slept with while the falling was occurring. Maybe that can help you trust me? It's not very reassuring, I suppose. I don't know what else to say. I hope that doesn't make you tell me no, though, because, Dylan, I *want* this. I want to learn from you. I want—"

He cut me off, crashing his mouth into mine. His lips were firm and persuasive, telling mine exactly where to move and what speed. Telling them when to open and take more. I responded eagerly, matching the strokes of his tongue with my own as soft whimpers escaped from my throat. My sounds made him groan and made me wet— wetter than I already was, that is. He swept me up with his kiss. He took me from the solid ground into a spiraling, dizzy windstorm.

He continued to hold my wrists above my head, which I found both highly erotic and frustrating at the same time. I wanted to caress his jaw. I wanted to slip my hands underneath his sweater. I wanted to draw the pads of my thumbs across his nipples and then trail my fingers down, down, down.

Unable to touch him the way I wanted, the rest of me

became more antsy beneath him, as though trying to make up for my restrained hands. I squirmed and bucked, trying to get as much of my body to come into contact with his as possible. But he counteracted every one of my moves, bracing his body higher above me, holding himself away.

It took me a few minutes to realize he was purposefully taunting me.

Then it took me another few minutes to realize I really liked this too. I mean, I hated it. But as the torture continued, a tension built inside me, low and deep. A hum that spread through my core and out to my limbs. By the time he lowered himself to grind across my crotch, I was already halfway to an orgasm.

From there, the hum intensified quickly. Each thrust of his pelvis against mine sent me closer to the edge. He still had his pants on! I still had on panties, and yet he'd found the perfect spot, hit it on every stroke, making the hum swell and expand and consume and take over and buzz, buzz, buzz, and…

Suddenly it was all gone at the sound of a clearing throat.

Guess when I'd sent the agent away I'd forgotten that he'd also be coming back.

Whoops.

I wasn't sorry. I wasn't sorry at all.

CHAPTER SEVEN

Dylan

I'd never lost an erection so fast.

Thank God, since it made it easier to scramble to my feet and distract Jeff Jones so Audrey could clothe herself privately. I was sweating and panicked as I diverted him back to the foyer. Behind me, I could hear the girl giggling.

It wasn't funny. It wasn't.

That she was laughing was a splendid example of why our age difference was a big problem. She was obviously not mature enough to handle matters that required adult responsibility. I was disappointed in myself for not being the adult from the start. If she hadn't been so tenacious, so assertive, so *beguiling*, I wouldn't have lost control of the situation.

And I *had* lost control. Really lost it. Almost gone too far, even.

The whole thing had left me flustered, and now there was a real chance I wasn't going to get this apartment.

"It's...I'm...this isn't at all what it looks like," I explained to the agent. I ran a hand through my hair, creating a floppy mess if I were to judge by the uneven way it felt on my scalp. "I sincerely apologize. It was inappropriate and discourteous and—"

"Just tell me one thing," Mr. Jones interrupted. "She's not really your daughter, is she?"

"No! God, no." I thought about it after I'd answered, what that must have looked like to the man when he'd walked in on us. It had been bad enough that we'd behaved so badly in an flat I hadn't yet leased. The fact that he'd also thought we were father and daughter was…

Well. Maybe it *was* funny.

"I'm sorry. I don't know why we said that she was." The grin that had slid onto my face made my latest apology seem insincere.

Fortunately, Jeff Jones was smiling too. "It's fine. I understand. I'm sure I'd play that game too if I were with a woman so…"

"Young?" Yes, I knew she was too young. He didn't need to throw it in my face.

"I was going to say willing. But maybe her youth has something to do with it." He peered over my shoulder, which made me have to glance behind me as well, insuring he wasn't seeing anything he shouldn't be seeing.

He wasn't. Audrey was dressed now and was simply straightening the tie of her wrap.

That didn't stop Jones from leering at her. "You're a very lucky man, Mr. Locke."

"Yes. I am," I said sternly, subtly enforcing a claim on her that I didn't have. His leer bothered me. A lot. I probably wouldn't have responded so possessively otherwise.

His smile faded, and the man looked appropriately cowed. He opened his mouth and closed it twice, as though trying to discern the best way to react.

I put him out of his misery and nodded at the file in his hands. "Are those the papers for the lease? Can I sign them now?"

"Oh! Yes. You may." He led me to the kitchen island where he spread out the contract in front of me. "Since we had you pre-approved before today, we've got all the finance and reference information that we need. You just need to initial the first two pages and put your John Hancock on the last, and I can hand over the keys right now."

He handed me a pen from inside the breast pocket of his jacket.

"And the terms of the contract are…?"

He used the pen to point to the paragraph answering my question. "Six months or until the unit is sold. If you're planning to purchase outright—"

"I am."

"—then you'll just want to make sure the sale goes through before the lease expires."

"I'll do that straight away." I took the pen and signed where he'd indicated.

When I was finished, Audrey sidled up next to me and clutched onto my arm. "Is it ours now?" she asked coyly.

I narrowed my eyes in her direction but didn't dispute the pretense that we were buying the flat together. It didn't feel necessary to confuse the agent any further, and besides, I was quite comfortable with the man believing Audrey was unavailable.

"Not quite yet, my dear, but we do get to have the keys now." I let the agent hand one to her so as not to destroy the latest ruse. I pocketed the duplicates. "Mr. Jones is going to put together an offer for us so we can buy the place outright."

"Sweet!" she exclaimed gazing up at me, and her eyes twinkled so spectacularly that I couldn't help imagining for a moment that we really were purchasing the place together. A pied-à-terre where I would teach her everything she wanted to know about her body and mine. As though she were a student, perhaps. The fantasy *was* "sweet." Delicious, even.

Too delectable to keep thinking about for too long.

I cleared my throat, forcing the fancy to dissipate from my head. "Do you need anything else from us?"

We briefly discussed an amount to offer the seller and decided the agent would pull up a few comps and get back to me before we confirmed the final number. I shook hands with him, watched with ire as he kissed the back of Audrey's hand, and then walked him to the door.

Once he was gone, I turned back to my companion and realized my mistake—I was again alone with Audrey. And this time there would be no one coming back to interrupt us.

Her expression said she'd realized the same thing. She didn't seem quite as upset about it as I was, though.

I thought quickly. "I shouldn't suggest this, but—"

"Yes. You should," she encouraged, stalking slowly toward me.

"Perhaps you'd like to join me somewhere for lunch."

Her face fell. "Oh. Then you aren't going to help me

out after all?"

Jesus, she was enchanting. Magnificently so. The pout of her mouth, the way her top lip formed a sharp V, the liquid almond of her eyes—it was impossible to deny her. I'd be a liar to say that I could.

"I'm not saying that. I just think this might be a task best suited for a different time. I'm picking up my son this afternoon, and I need to stop by the office to chat with Nate and Weston and Donovan about a few things while we're all in the same place. Also, I have to bring my belongings from the hotel to the flat. Surely you have plans with Sabrina."

She let out a loud sigh, not unlike the teenage sighs I heard often enough from Aaron. "We're seeing a Broadway show tonight. I'm supposed to meet her at the office around four."

"Good. That leaves us time for lunch." I pulled her coat from the cupboard and helped her put it on. "We can work out an arrangement for the, er, the other thing from there."

She linked her arm through mine and beamed up at me. "Sounds like a plan, professor."

My trousers tightened at her newest title for me. Daddy? Professor? Did she know she'd hit the bullseye on my hot buttons?

If she didn't, her naivety certainly added to her allure.

And if she *did* know, as I expected she did, I had to wonder—what exactly could she possibly learn from me?

"I knew it would happen one day, honestly. He's a teenager

now. He wants to spend his school breaks on skiing trips with his friends and playing marathon sessions of Fortnite, or whatever the game is he's into at the moment. He doesn't want to waste half of his holidays stuck in an aeroplane traveling to visit his boring old father." I paused to take a swallow of my champagne. It was early for alcohol, but Audrey had said the finding of my apartment had warranted a celebration, and as I'd already discovered, it was impossible to deny her whims.

Which was also why I'd spent the last ten minutes waxing on about Aaron. What a boring subject for a young female companion. Nothing could bring out the old man in me like reminding me of my teenager. I knew better than to bring up the topic, but as soon as the waiter had taken our order, she'd asked.

And she was compelling, that one was. She didn't have to ask twice.

To her credit, she'd remained engaged throughout my indulgent rant, asking questions, adding commentary. "He's so young," she said now—ironically, I thought. "This is just a phase of growing up. I remember feeling the same way at that age—not about my father. He died when I was thirteen. And then Sabrina left school to look after me, and I remember feeling so smothered. Like, I knew she'd sacrificed for me, and that should make me more appreciative, but I was a total pain in her behind. I resented her, for some reason. I didn't want her around. I mean, I *did*, but I didn't act like I did. I grew out of it—mostly. Aaron will too."

She really was lovely. Giving me advice on my son, who I felt more and more out of touch with as the years went by, was not something I expected at all in exchange for my help with her situation.

No, my reward for that was simply being the man she'd chosen as her tutor.

"He will. I know he will," I agreed. My stepdaughter had been the same way. At the time it had been hard to distinguish whether it was an age-related behavior or if it had been caused by my intrusion into her life. Amanda and I had gotten along well, but a new stepfather is always an adjustment.

I tapped my finger along the rim of the champagne glass. "Why do you think children resent the elders caring for them? Is there some secret club that requires that as an initiation into adulthood that I don't remember?"

She laughed. "Actually, sort of yes. You hit puberty, and your body is suddenly an adult body, which doesn't mean you make adult choices yet, but you *think* you do. And here's this person who—in my case—isn't much older than you, and she's in charge of all the rules, and some of them are ridiculous, and you know that she's wrong about everything, even if she did set her future aside to be there for you, and how can you not resent that? Then you grow up a little more and realize, oh, fudge. She was right about almost everything."

She ran her tongue over her bottom lip and brought her point back to me. "In your case, you don't live with Aaron every day. Yet you still have automatic authority over him, and he has to believe he knows better than you. And maybe he does sometimes, but he can't possibly realize all the times he doesn't. All you can do is give him lots of space to express what he feels. And then more space to let him feel it. And all the while you'll be there, hanging back, but close enough to protect him if he needs it."

"Sage advice." I meant it too. She was as wise as she was dear, it appeared. "I hope that's exactly what I'm doing with buying the flat. I don't want to force him to be with me, but I still want to be near him, when I can. I'll come for Christmas and spring break, and I'll spend as much of the summer as I can over here. It's only three years until he graduates from high school, and if he decides he really wants to go to NYU like he says he wants to, then he'll have a place to live that isn't with his mother. It would be cruel to expect him to live with that monster a minute longer than he has to."

Usually I wasn't that awful about Ellen to other people, particularly people who were practically strangers, but Audrey was a good listener, and I was not on the best terms with my ex as of late. The chance to be honest was simultaneously refreshing and concerning.

Audrey's eyebrows rose. "A monster? So she's the awful creature that poisoned you into believing you had to be a pessimist to survive the world."

"I'm not a pessimist—I'm a realist. I'm sure it's difficult to tell the difference when you're as unrealistically optimistic as you are—"

"Hey, now!"

I smiled to let her know I was teasing. Mostly. "But I promise you that the glasses I'm looking through are quite clear. There was no poison except truth."

"The worst poison of all." Her cheeks were pink and her eyes bright, and I suspected she was yanking my chain, but it was hard to care. Her attention was pleasant enough to make up for any mocking.

She must have felt guilty for it, though, because she grew serious then. "I'm sorry. I don't know her at all. Or your situation. She's probably a terrible beast. I can't imagine any other reason a woman wouldn't get along with you."

And now *I* felt guilty.

"No, she wasn't a terrible beast. Not really." Even with her affairs, even though she'd stopped loving me long before I'd stopped loving her. "She was broken and in grief, and it's easier to believe that she was a shitty human being rather than facing the fact that I couldn't make things better for her. That I wasn't a strong enough anchor to hold onto her. That I hadn't loved her enough to replace the things she'd lost."

I'd never said that before. Not out loud. Not really to myself, even, except in the wake of consuming several glasses of bourbon.

Audrey blinked at me sympathetically. "Wow. That's heavy. Does it feel good to be able to admit that?"

"No." It *didn't* feel good. It felt extremely shitty, but it did feel authentic, and that felt meaningful. "I'm glad I said it, though." I threw back the rest of my champagne, hoping to cover up the awkward aftertaste of my confession.

When that didn't work, I deflected. "And now it seems you know the source of my bitterness, what's the source of your *not*-bitterness?"

"My parents," she said quickly.

This surprised me, mostly because I hadn't expected she'd have an answer at all.

"My father, actually," she corrected herself. "I was only nine when my mother died, so memories of her and them together is a bit hazy, but what I do remember is how much he loved her. How he doted on her and took care of her and adored her, even after her death. He had such respect and devotion for her ghost that it almost felt like she was still there when she'd gone. He kept her present. He didn't date after her, and he had every reason to be sad and miserable without her—raising two girls on his own, especially—but his love for her kept him happy and upbeat right up until he passed himself."

I scrutinized her as I carefully framed what I wanted to say in my head. How could I present my view while still being delicate about treading on her childlike notions about what went on in someone else's relationship? "You don't think that you could be romanticizing their relationship? As you said, thirteen is awfully young…" I knew it came out patronizing even when I'd intended it not to.

Or, perhaps that's what I'd exactly intended. Whether her parents had actually had a magical marriage or not, she obviously believed that it was the ultimate goal. She didn't realize those relationships were not typical, and that she could love and dote and devote herself to the man of her dreams, and he would still shit all over her.

She needed saving from her fairy-tale notions.

But was I the hero for being the asshole who exposed the reality of her sweet memories?

She didn't fall for it for a minute.

"There he is!" She pointed at me while giving me a toothy grin. "There's the man I met last night. You've been almost likable all afternoon. I was beginning to wonder if your curmudgeon behavior had all been an act." She clapped her hands together suddenly. "You know what it is? I'm good for you! I bring out the best in you. How lucky you met me!"

How lucky I met her? "Humbug," I said. But it was impossible not to smile.

And as long as I was being authentic, as long as I was

being honest, she did bring out the best in me. She reminded me of that pure passion I'd felt for life so long ago. It
was nice to remember that man I'd once been, even if it
wasn't a man I ever wanted to be again.

But she was wrong on one point—it wasn't *good* for
me. *She* wasn't good for me. To believe she was would be
an absolute lie.

CHAPTER EIGHT

Audrey

DYLAN: Are you still awake?
My pulse picked up at the message from Dylan when it arrived. It was half past midnight, and I'd texted him hours ago during the intermission of *Waitress*. I'd been antsy waiting for a response, afraid he was bailing on me, so obviously, I was relieved to see his name, to say the least.

Now was a better time to talk to him anyway. Sabrina was already asleep, and I wasn't as into my reading of *A Curator's Handbook* as I should have been.

But I *was* into Dylan Locke. *More* than I should have been.

AUDREY: I was beginning to think u'd gotten cold feet.

DYLAN: Ha ha. No. Not particularly. It was a lot of rigamarole to get

the flat ready for habitation, even
though it came furnished. Then Aaron
and I had to battle through Latin
homework. After that, we ordered piz-
za and played a rousing game of Risk.

I giggled. He was so formal and long-winded in his
messages. No one spoke like that in text. No one used
proper grammar. But *he* did. He texted like he talked. I'd
probably make fun of him about it someday—I was known
to tease—but secretly I loved it. It was old-fashioned and
charming.

I curled my feet underneath me in Sabrina's guest room
armchair and typed out a response.

AUDREY: Risk, huh. He let u win,
didn't he?

DYLAN: Now that you mention it...I
really think he did.

I could picture it—a baby teenage boy, awkward and
gangly after a recent growth spurt, chocolate eyes like his
father, a dry but still underdeveloped sense of humor. The
two would crack witty wisecracks while forming armies
and taking over the world, and Dylan would be so enam-
ored with the idea of connecting with his son, he wouldn't
see that the same son was throwing the game.

It was a sweet image, and even if it was inaccurate, I
liked imagining it that way. It made me miss my dad who'd
died ten years ago this holiday season. I had fond memories of nights when it was just the two of us. Years after my
mother had died when Sabrina had gone off to school at
Harvard. Nights playing Rummikub past midnight. After
I'd win a handful of games, I'd start losing on purpose so

my father would stay interested in playing.

Those were good times.

These were beautiful moments Dylan was creating, too. Did he know that? He had to assume they had some meaning. Why else be so engaged? Why else buy an apartment he only planned on using a handful of times a year? He was a very wealthy businessman, a man I suspected that could afford staff and "people" to look after all his needs. He probably lived quite a different life when he was back home in London, but here, where his son was concerned, he seemed very ordinary. He was just like most dads. He cared about his kid, and it showed.

It made me want to care too. It made me want to ask too many questions and get involved.

But that was always my problem—I cared too easily. And this wasn't a situation where caring helped me.

I blew the air from my lungs and shook my head free from sentimental thoughts. Yes, Dylan was a good dad. But I needed to focus on the kind of "daddy" he could be to me.

This was a conversation I decided would be best voice-to-voice.

I hit the phone icon next to his name and put the receiver up to my ear.

And then I waited.

And waited.

He made me wait four flipping rings before answering. Four long rings where I pictured him staring at my name on his screen and panicking, trying to decide what to do.

Answer it, you nincompoop! You were just texting me! I know you're there!

"Audrey," he said in a stern bass when he finally picked

up. It made my stomach buzz deep and low, as though trying to match his pitch and resonance.

"Dylan," I said, in kind.

Then neither of us said anything and silence stretched out between us.

It wasn't awkward silence, really, but it was noticeable. Noticeable enough that my lips went dry, and my hands began to sweat. It seemed to me it was his turn to say something since I'd just spoken, whatever it was that I'd said. I'd already forgotten. I was too consumed with replaying the way he'd said my name. How beautiful it sounded when he said it in his very British dialect. It made me feel regal and classic and adored, which was crazy since we were practically strangers.

But I felt that way all the same.

And I sat there without speaking as I soaked it in. I didn't know what *his* reason was for not talking, but that was mine.

"*You* called *me*," he said eventually. "I believe you have the obligation to do the talking here, Audrey."

That answered that question. And he'd said my name again, and I felt heady.

But I got my act together, somehow. "Yes. Right! I wanted to tell you that I can be there in half an hour. Sooner if you don't mind getting me in my pajamas. What I wear shouldn't really matter since the clothes won't be on long anyway. Unless that's not how you do things. Do you keep your clothes on and just uncover the necessary part? That does sound hot, in a way. Maybe the secret to all my bad sex was getting naked?"

"Bad sex from getting naked? No. I don't think that's it. I've done both with the same results. I expect we'll see what...hold on. Hold on. What am I even saying?" He sounded flustered, like he always was when I threw myself at him. I found that part charming as well. "Audrey, it's nearly one in the morning. And Aaron is still here. He's sleeping right now, but I don't think it would be appropriate to have a late-night visitor of the female persuasion."

Yeah, probably not.

"Or any persuasion, for that matter. Ellen would have my hide, and the whole purpose of getting this flat was to make things easier between all of us, not more strained."

"Fine," I said, laying as much disappointment as possible into the single syllable.

He let out a slow breath, and I pictured him running a hand through his hair as he did. I'd seen him do it on more than one occasion, and now it had become A Very Dylan gesture in my mind.

"What's your day look like tomorrow?" he asked.

It was my turn to sigh. "Tomorrow's terrible. Well, not terrible, really. Terrible for the two of us getting together, though. Sabrina took the day off to take me around the city. And then we're seeing the Rockettes' Christmas show. It's going to be jam-packed with holiday fun. Woot! Oh, hey! Maybe you could come up with some project she needs to take care of at the office, and make her have to cancel her plans so she can come in and work."

"I can't possibly do that. I'm not in her direct chain of command. I don't even work in the same office. Not to mention the questionable judgement of ethics required to use my authority over her simply to arrange a booty call. And you can't tell me you don't want to spend time with your sister. You came here for Thanksgiving break to be with her, not with…" He paused and seemed to come to his senses. "I see now. You were winding me up."

I bit my lip to stifle a laugh. "I was totally 'winding you up.'" I was also keeping that phrase and using it forever and ever. "But I'm thoroughly impressed with your moral code. You're a good man, Dylan Locke."

"Or, at least, I'm a gullible one." He laughed softly. "Then if the daytime is off the table, that leaves the night. I'm meeting with some old friends for dinner so I won't have Aaron. I don't imagine we'll go too late, and I can cut it short if need be. Will you be too tired to make a trip over here after your show?"

"Uh, I'm a college student. All-nighters are kind of my gig. The question is—will it be a problem for you, old man?"

"You like to remind me of our age difference, I think." I could practically hear his scowl through the line.

"Only because it makes you so hot and bothered."

"Does it make *you* hot and bothered?" His voice had dropped and the words that came out were ragged.

"Yes, Professor Locke." My answer sounded just as raw as the question, and the buzz in my belly had spread out through my limbs. It made me hotter the more I thought I about it.

"Let me ask you then—as your professor, I should know what sort of prior education you've acquired."

Oh, geez. He was always incredibly sexy, but he was even hotter when he played the teacher part. Especially when he was also enthusiastic.

"Um." I stood up to pace the room, hoping to release some of the restlessness he stirred in me. "Let's see."

"If you're uncomfortable discussing this—"

"I'm not," I cut him off. "At all. I just know our time is limited, and I have a lot to learn."

"I find it hard to believe that you are truly that inexperienced. Why don't you just lay it all out, and I can decide what would be most useful for us to focus on?"

I got the sense that he wasn't so much feeling me out as he was feeling himself out. Trying to decide if he was really up for what I wanted of him.

It was probably a cue for me to proceed cautiously.

But cautious wasn't my nature. "Okay, then. I'm pretty sure I'm good on blowjobs. I can deepthroat and swallow and I know the tricks about humming and using a peppermint lifesaver at the same time. And I've never had any complaints in that area, but if you think you might have something to teach me… I'm terrible at receiving oral sex, on the other hand. I can't ever decide if it feels good or just weird, and that makes me tense, and I never come. And positions. I've done missionary practically every time. Oh, and cowgirl—or whatever it's called when the girl is on top. But I don't think I know how to do that right because I've heard that it should be easier to orgasm that way, and I never have. I've never orgasmed at all, actually. Not from a guy, anyway. I mean, I've come on my own, but isn't sex supposed to be better with someone else? I'd really like to figure out how to make it better with someone else."

I bit my bottom lip and waited, sure that what I'd said would wind him up.

That was part of the fun of Dylan, after all.

"That's. Hm." He cleared his throat. "That's quite a list of concerns."

"Told you." I flopped down on the bed and put my feet flat on the headboard. "Am I unhelpable? Is it humiliating that my education is so sparse that I can't even orgasm with a guy?"

"That's not a problem with your education—that's a problem with the men you've been with. *They* should be humiliated. Truly."

Maybe it was flattery, but he didn't have to try to get in my pants. And Dylan was generally earnest. He meant what he said, and his show of support made my insides feel warm and twisted. Not to mention wet.

Kind as it was, it also didn't fix my situation. "Thank you for that. I appreciate it, I do. But it's still a problem for me, even if it isn't my fault. So I'll teach the next guy. No big deal. Just...how can I teach a guy what to do if I don't know what I like myself?"

"Then we have to figure out what you like. And teach you how to ask for it."

Yes. That. "Mr. Locke, I think we're on the same page. Does this help you with your lesson plan?"

"I believe it does."

He was so solemn that I couldn't help poking at him. "You know, I'm grateful you're taking this project seriously, for my sake. But it's okay if you enjoy it, too."

He let out a gruff laugh that made goosebumps scatter down my arms. "I'll have you know that I'm enjoying this very much. Now, you might not need much sleep, but I'd better get some if I'm expected to be at my best for you. I'll see you tomorrow night, sweet girl."

"Good night, Professor." I clicked the button to end the call and stretched my hands over my head in giddy victory.

Humming to myself, I set the phone on the nightstand, turned off the lamp, and climbed under the covers. I was all talk about all-nighters. In truth, I liked my sleep.

But I sat awake for a long time, smiling in the dark, as I thought about all the possible ways Dylan would *enjoy* me.

I got trapped.

After a full day of sightseeing and holiday activities, I'd figured that Sabrina would want to call it a night as soon as the Rockettes' show was over. Especially since she was also exhausted from the emotional turbulence of her relationship with Donovan Kincaid.

Unfortunately, she'd gotten a second wind right as the curtains closed, and instead of going straight back to her apartment like I'd hoped, we ended up at a Don't Tell Mama's until almost two in the morning.

I might have tried to persuade her that I was tired, but she knew me better than that. And she needed to have a good time, a night where she could unload all her worry on me. I rarely got to be the comforter between the two of us. She was my sister, but in many ways she was also my mother. Even when I wanted to be there for her, she rarely allowed it.

This time it was Dylan who texted to check in on me. Not wanting to divert my attention away from Sabrina, I hadn't gotten a chance to reply until Sabrina and I were in our separate rooms back at her place.

AUDREY: I just got home! I'm so sorry! Is it too late to come over?

I wasn't even sure he'd answer at this time of night, and if he did, I was certain he'd want to reschedule.

But I was wrong.

DYLAN: No worries. I got a nap in
this afternoon. But I don't want you
taking an Uber at this time of night.
I'll send my car for you. Text me
when you're in my lobby so I know
you've arrived safely.

He "got a nap." I chuckled out loud. Either he was taking this project ultra seriously, or he was winding *me* up
for a change. I had a feeling both were likely.

And he was sending me his car—that was...nice. Really nice. Make-my-heart-flip-in-my-chest kind of nice.
He was essentially a stranger and still he cared about my
safety. I'd practically been engaged to my last boyfriend,
Mateo, and he'd never been the slightest bit concerned
about me walking around late at night after study sessions.
Certainly a university campus was at least as dangerous as
a sidewalk in Midtown for a girl like me.

Grateful and glad that our plans were still on, I threw
Dylan a quick text back before slipping out of Sabrina's
apartment.

AUDREY: Thanks for looking out for
me, Daddy. ;)

His reply came when I was in the elevator.

DYLAN: I sense teasing in your last
message.

And another followed right after, one that instantly
made me feel the most taboo kind of sexy.

DYLAN: Be careful. Daddy only rewards

girls who show him respect.

Oh, boy. Dylan was good.

When I got to the lobby of Sabrina's building, I realized exactly how good he was—the car was already waiting for me. He must have had it on standby, ready for whenever I finally got back to him.

The ride to Dylan's apartment was quick with the late-night quiet—eh, quiet*er*—streets. I hummed Christmas songs from the show as we drove, and even though I still had the key Jeff Jones had given me, I texted Dylan as soon as I got there to let him know I'd arrived like he'd asked. The key got me in the front door without trouble and into the elevator, so I was bouncing down the hallway toward his unit in a matter of minutes.

All of it had happened so fast, in fact, that it wasn't until I was outside his door with the key in my hand, lifted toward the lock, that I thought to step back and take a moment. It wasn't that I had doubts about my plan—I didn't. Not a one. And I didn't have doubts about Dylan either. He was everything I wanted in a teacher. He was kind and protective and level-headed. Most importantly, he was out-of-this-world attractive. The apex of my thighs felt slippery just from the thought of being with him.

But there was me to think about. Who I was and what kind of reactions I usually had to men I was into. I fell for them, was what I did. Over and over. I'd only had two serious boyfriends in my life, but the number of guys I'd been smitten with was countless. I easily swooned over kind gestures. Butterflies resided in my stomach at all times. If a man looked too long in my eyes, laughed at my stupid jokes, or listened attentively to my rants about art, he was sure to win my heart.

The only reason I'd survived as long as I had in the world—if twenty-three was considered having survived long at all—was because I also had a level head. Because I knew not to run blindly into the arms of every guy who gave me goosebumps. Because I'd learned to tuck my feelings deep inside. I'd perfected the art of not being vulnerable, partly by making sure I didn't jump into bed with anyone until I was sure he loved me too.

Everything about this situation with Dylan was against the Audrey Lind Code of Conduct.

So how on earth did I expect to get through this without getting burned?

The same way you always do. That was how.

I'd remind myself of the facts—that Dylan wasn't emotionally available. That he lived across an ocean. That he wasn't interested in any relationship with me or anyone, for that matter. I'd repeat those facts over and over until they were seared into my brain, and when I started to feel—which was highly likely considering my past—I'd bury those feelings and never mention them out loud. Then, after a while, a new guy would cross my path, and I'd get all twitterpated again and the cycle would continue until eventually I found the *right* guy. And finally I wouldn't have to hide anymore.

It would happen. I believed it with all of me. And this thing with Dylan was preparing me for being ready for that guy, and it was important. And logical. And I would survive this way until that future arrived.

With my pep talk completed, I threw my shoulders back, inserted the key in the lock, and swung open the door.

Before I even had time to cross the threshold, I was grabbed by the wrist, pulled into the foyer, and pushed against the wall.

"You hesitated in the hall," Dylan said, his mouth at my ear, his voice husky. He'd shut the door with his foot, and now the length of his body was crushed against mine. "Are you having second thoughts?"

The light was off in the foyer, and except for the moonlight that shone in from the front room, it was dark. But I didn't need to see to be able to tell how much Dylan hoped that I wasn't reconsidering our arrangement. His eagerness was evident from the thick ridge pressing against my lower belly.

"No second thoughts," I assured him. "I was just pulling myself together."

His lips hovered along the curve of my jaw. "You can still back out of this. At any time. You just say the word, and everything stops."

The only word I wanted to say at this moment was "Don't." Don't stop. Don't back out of this. Don't make me wait a second longer.

But I was speechless. My heart was in my throat, hammering away at my vocal cords. A shiver ran through my body, despite the heavy coat I was wearing. I licked my lips, inviting his mouth to cover mine. I willed it with all my being. *Kiss me. Kiss me!*

"Tell me you understand," he insisted.

I dropped the key and my purse to the floor and swept the palms of my hands up his torso, over his shirt. "I get it. Please, don't stop. Please—"

He cut me off with a kiss, immediately deep and frantic. Without breaking his mouth from mine, he undid the buttons of my coat and pushed it off my shoulders, letting it join my other belongings on the ground. Then he shoved closer against me, inhabiting the space the bulky coat had previously owned.

My chest rose and fell rapidly, the bullet points of my nipples brushing against him with each breath. I threw my arms around his neck and silently begged for more—more contact, more kissing, more of all of this.

It was happening. Really happening, and already it was so thrilling and charged that I was absolutely sure I wouldn't retain anything that I learned. What's more, I didn't even care. Screw the lessons. I just wanted him to screw me.

Thankfully, Dylan still had his head about him. "Without speaking, tell me what you want."

"But I...I don't know, remember? I..."

He amended. "Show me where you need to be touched. I know you need it, you saucy girl. Show me where your body aches for my hands."

I couldn't think. I didn't know. But I closed my eyes, and I could feel the heaviness of my breasts and the aching of my nipples and the buzzing from below, between my thighs. I arched my back, pushing my chest toward him.

"You need my hands on your tits, don't you, sweet girl?"

He was already undoing the top buttons of my shirt dress, but I nodded anyway. "I do. I do!"

"Shh. I know." He kissed me quickly, then pulled back to watch as his hands drew my dress open. He hadn't removed my belt or undone any of the buttons below that, so the top only fell down to my elbows, trapping my arms from excessive movement and revealing my bra and the globes trapped beneath the white lace.

He stared hungrily as he brushed his knuckles across my decolletage, so close—but not close enough—to where he'd correctly identified I needed him. Such a good professor. I arched my back again, reminding him, and he chuckled. Then, with one swift movement, he tugged both bra cups down, exposing my breasts and my embarrassingly erect nipples.

And finally—*finally*—he touched them, scissoring my nipples with his fingers as he filled his palms with the fatty flesh. I let out a whimper, but leaned into him, asking for more. His pinch tightened, bringing me to the balls of my feet with a full moan.

Dylan kissed me and whispered praises. Praises that I couldn't quite make out over the increasing buzz between my legs. It was loud and urgent, demanding attention. I wriggled, rubbing my thighs together, seeking relief.

"Show me." Dylan's harsh command cut through the haze, prompting me once again to tell him where I needed to be touched.

I stepped a foot on either side of one of his and bucked my hips forward. He bent his knee, and now I could ride him they way I wanted, rubbing my pussy against him, showing him where I ached.

"Good girl," his voice rumbled, gathering my dress around my waist. "Good girl for showing me where you need me."

Instead of touching me there, though, he slid his hands down inside my leggings to palm my behind. It was torture, feeling the burn of his skin against mine while elsewhere I was on fire from the absence of his caress.

But then his hands were inching lower, down into the crease between my cheeks. "No knickers," he said in a hiss. "You are as much of a bad girl as you are a good one, aren't you, Audrey?"

Really, it had been about pantylines. Tight leggings show everything, and I wasn't fond of thongs.

But before I could respond, he dug his fingers into my flesh and pulled me forward, bringing his knee up tight against my pussy at the same time. The increase in friction took the buzz from mono to stereo. I put my hands flat against the wall behind me for support as my mouth parted in a desperate sigh.

There were more murmurs from Dylan, more sighs from me, and then he was pulling my leggings down to my thighs, exposing the recently trimmed (thank heavens) patch of hair above my naughty bits, to borrow the British term. I spread my legs farther, unabashedly. Showing him. Begging him.

And somehow he knew.

Because his fingers found his way between my pussy lips, and with expertise, he strummed my skin, he stoked the fire, until fireworks were going off in front of my eyes and my head was spinning in circles, and I was clutching onto him while the most beautiful, most tremulous climax wracked through my body.

Oh, my. Oh, wow. That was…it was *everything*. It was ecstasy and paradise and yes, oh, yes, sex was definitely better with another person. Dizzying and delicious and divine.

Slowly, I came to my senses again, and I realized Dylan was kissing my jaw and stroking the delicate skin above my clit, easing me back to reality.

I moved my hands up his arms and braced them on his shoulders, steadying me as I looked into his eyes. I had to tell him how good it had been, how perfect. How monumental.

But all that came out was, "I liked that."

He laughed lightly. "Which part?"

"All of it. Every single bit." I couldn't narrow it down if I'd tried. I'd been too captivated by feeling to even know what had happened.

Which was entirely beyond the point of this exercise. I needed to be able to recall every detail. "What did you do?"

He leaned back to study my face. "Can you stand through another one?"

"I think so." My legs were wobbly, but I had the wall at my back, and Dylan to help keep me up.

"Then this time I'll tell you. Try to pay attention." He moved his hands back to my breasts, plumping them. "I watched how your body leaned into me. I watched where. Those were the parts of you begging for attention."

He pinched my nipples now, light at first, then, when I moaned, harder.

He waited for me to quiet before going on, his voice so low it was almost a whisper. "I listened to your whimpers. If you'd backed away, I would have known it was too much. But you arched your back toward me. So I gave you more."

He continued this way, easing through each of the same movements as before, showing me how he decided he'd touch me based on my reactions. Teaching me that I was the one who ran the show. All he had to do, he said, was observe. Observe how my breaths grew shallow the closer I got to orgasm. Observe how my grip got tighter on his shirt. Observe how my eyelids fluttered and my head fell back.

I heard him talking. I heard what he was saying, but also I didn't. I was whirling again in a second, more powerful climax. I exploded like a bomb, shaking and crying out with volatile pleasure. It was agony. It was rapture. It was fire and ice and everything in between.

And I knew—absolutely without a doubt knew—that I was in trouble.

Not only because I was bound to become very fond of this man—more likely, it had already happened, and I just hadn't admitted it—but also because I was one thousand percent certain that whatever it was that he'd done to me—twice now!—couldn't be taught to someone else. It was a skill. It was a talent. Something a person was born with or wasn't. Maybe it could be honed, but only if there was already a natural inclination and a desire to please, and I'd never dated a man like that before. Never dated a man with those gifts.

I couldn't teach this to a lover.

Dylan Locke was meant to make things better. Instead, he'd ruined me forever.

CHAPTER NINE

Dylan

I was caught. Ensnared in her net. I'd taken the bait, and after one sweet taste, I was captured. There was nothing left for me to do but surrender, let her cut me open and skin me. Let her feast.

I'd never guessed that my end would be so inviting, yet here it was, so delicious and tempting.

After watching her beautifully fall apart—not once, but twice—I knew there would be no sleeping that night. I had to have her in every way. I'd devour her, let myself be devoured, until dawn, if she let me. We still hadn't made it past the foyer. There were so many places left in my flat to defile her, and I planned to take advantage of them all.

I pressed tightly against her, grinding the steel rod in my trousers into the softness of her belly while I kissed her with abandon. With one hand braced on her hip, another cupped under her chin, I anchored myself in the moment, ignoring the nagging worry about tomorrow and the late hour and the incessant vibration of my phone in my pocket, and kissed her so deeply I lost myself.

"What is that?" she asked, breaking away suddenly. "What is that buzzing against me? Do you have a vibrator in there?" She moved her hands down to my trousers and reached, not for the aching rod of my cock, but into my pocket.

Then she withdrew my phone, still buzzing, the screen lit up brightly in the darkness with a single name—Ellen.

It should have been Hell-en. That would have been more fitting considering the moment she seemed desperate to destroy. She was, in every way, a devil.

The ringing ended and the screen showed I'd had six missed calls. A second past and it began buzzing again.

That's when I came to my wits.

Ellen calling, late at night, over and over—it had to be Aaron.

I snatched the phone from Audrey's hand and answered it as I brought it to my ear. "What's wrong?"

"Thank God you finally answered. I didn't remember you being such a sound sleeper." Ellen sounded both worked up and accusing.

I had no interest in addressing the latter. "Tell me what's wrong."

"It's Aaron. He's not in his room. I can't find him."

Cold panic washed over me replacing the heat that had blazed through my veins only minutes before. I stepped away from Audrey and ran a hand through the flop of my hair. "What do you mean you can't find him? It's—" I glanced at my watch. "Nearly three in the morning. Where the hell would he have gone?"

"I don't know, Dylan!" She was terrified. I could hear

it in the shrill pitch of her voice. Ellen was never terrified. She was cool as a cucumber, that one. Her agitation fed mine, urging me to act.

"I'll be right there. Ring the police." I glanced at Audrey and found her already putting herself together, hiding away the soft silk of her luscious breasts, covering the damp curls of her stunning pussy.

"I already have. Please, hurry," Ellen said, and I hated her in this moment more than I'd hated her in years. Hated the reminder that we still shared our son, though we'd never share anything else again. Hated that she'd asked me nicely, as though she assumed I had a choice in my own child's safety. Hated the intrusion of harsh reality into my perfect lie of a fantasy.

I hung up on her in reply.

Without pause, I headed straight to the coat cupboard and pulled out the cashmere Ted Baker hanging inside. I put it on, then turned back to my guest. She was just slipping an arm through her own coat. I rushed to help her, brushing her long caramel hair off her shoulder before moving to button her up.

"I'm sorry," I said, wishing I had time for other words, sweeter words. She deserved better than this.

She shook her head adamantly. "No, you have to go. I get it." She brought her hand up to stroke her knuckles against my cheek.

I caught her hand as she dropped it and brought it to my mouth to kiss her palm. "I'm still sorry. There's so much more…" I closed my eyes, forcing away the thoughts of all the *more* I'd meant to address with her this night. When I opened them again, I couldn't look directly at her. "I'll walk down with you."

We were silent in the lift. I was too worried, too frantic, too furious at Ellen to make conversation. Whether Audrey was respectful of my situation or peeved about the interruption to our plans, I wasn't sure. I didn't allow myself to think about it. I could only think about Aaron.

Halfway across the lobby, I stopped suddenly. "What am I thinking? You need a ride." I pulled out my phone and dialed my driver.

Audrey put a hand up as though to stop me. "I can Uber. You take the car."

"It will be faster if I walk. It's only a couple of blocks. I'd prefer if—" I cut off when the driver answered the line. "Yes, she's ready to be picked up now. Same address as earlier." He gave me an estimated time of arrival, and I hung up.

"He'll be here in seven minutes." I looked out the front doors to the snowy street beyond then back at my companion, longingly. "I wish I could stay."

"No, please don't. Go. Text me when you find him safe." A thought seemed to occur to her. "Oh, and Dylan. When you find him...listen to what he has to say. Kids don't usually do crazy things like this without a reason, as silly as their reasons might seem."

My brow furrowed as I endured her advice. I didn't generally like counsel without invitation, particularly from someone without any kids of her own.

She sensed she'd overstepped. "I'm sorry. It's not my place. Just...it wasn't that long ago that I was sneaking out of my house, and I thought I could help."

She was genuine and utterly enchanting, and I realized, I wasn't bothered after all by her intrusion. I was _grateful_.

I wanted to kiss her for it. Because she had perfect

plump lips. Because she tasted like honey. Because she was warm and the night was cold, and I'd been in the dark for so long.

But casual kissing wasn't what we were about, and I was in a rush, so I nodded my goodbye, and dashed out the door.

It took less than ten minutes to walk from my building to Ellen's. The doorman let me through, having been alerted that both I and the police would be arriving. When I got to her unit, I rapped quietly on the door, aware of the wee hour of the night.

She answered right away, ushering me in quickly.

"Tell me what happened," I ordered, already heading to Aaron's room to see for myself that he was indeed not there.

She followed after me, tripping over herself to keep up with my wide gait. "He went to his room right after dinner, around seven, saying he had homework he wanted to get done ahead of the weekend. I did some work, changed into my pajamas, then curled up with a glass of wine in the living room to watch a holiday thing on Netflix. I meant to check on him when I went to bed, but I guess I fell asleep, and when I woke up, I looked then, and he was gone."

"So you have no idea how long he'd been missing?"

"No. But I couldn't have fallen asleep before nine-thirty or ten. It was probably after that when he…"

Unless he'd snuck out before then, while she wasn't paying attention.

New York flats being what they were, it only took a second to verify Aaron's absence. I turned to my ex-wife, looking at her for the first time since I'd arrived. She was wearing a long sheer nightgown with a silk robe that nearly reached her feet.

She'd never worn anything that fancy to bed when we'd been married.

I took a step toward her. "You were alone all evening?" I meant to sound as accusatory as I did.

"What are you asking?" She clutched the lapels of her robe like she did to her defenses.

"You're sure you weren't entertaining a male gentleman and that's why you didn't realize our son had disappeared before three in the goddamned morning?"

"As though it couldn't happen on your watch."

"I find it hard to believe I wouldn't notice a thirteen-year-old boy sneaking out of a flat this size. It's not like this is Grand Central Station, for Christ's sake. It's not even two thousand square feet."

She stuck her chin out. "Really? You'd notice? Like how you noticed your wife had been having affairs for nearly a year before you confronted her about it?"

Splice. Right through the skin, straight to the heart. She knew where to hit me, how to strike with her words. I *hadn't* noticed her affairs. I hadn't wanted to.

And maybe she was showing me something of herself too—that she'd *wanted* me to notice, and I hadn't. She'd wanted me to save her, and I couldn't. Another reminder of how I'd failed her. How I'd failed all of us.

See that, Audrey? Love doesn't win. It just disappoints. Over and over again.

"Mom? Dad? What's going on?" The thin voice in the doorway pulled our focus immediately.

There he was, still bundled in his coat and a beanie cap that said *Excelsior!* in bold red letters across the front.

God, we were both shitty parents—Ellen and I. So wrapped up in ourselves and the same old argument that we couldn't even notice the kid we were looking for when he came home.

"Aaron!" Ellen ran to him, enveloping him in her arms. "You're here! You're all right! We were so worried! We called the police and your dad came over and I was out of my mind…"

Her relief at his appearance quickly faded and the anxiety of the night crept in to take its place. She pulled out of her embrace and gripped him tightly by the upper arms. "Where the hell have you been, young man? How dare you frighten us like that!"

"I went out!" he answered defiantly.

"To that damn YouTube meetup with your friends, didn't you? The one I said absolutely not to when you asked if you could go?"

His guilty expression told the answer as much as his silence.

I hung back and watched, my own relief seeping in slowly and heavily, trapping me like quicksand. What could have happened? What might have been? This late on the streets of a busy city. Barely a teenager.

It was easier not to think about. Easier to just watch and sink.

They made an odd tableau, the two of them. Ellen, who stood on the upper side of average, barraging Aaron, who nearly stood as tall as she did these days, with her verbal onslaught. How long before she lost all control over him? Soon, if she wasn't careful. Soon if she hadn't already.

But could I even judge her parenting? Was I any better of a father, absent as I was? And, truth be told, I would have been yelling myself hoarse if she hadn't taken the lead. If I weren't drowning in my emotions. If I weren't remembering Audrey's last words to me—*Listen to what he has to say.*

So far, he hadn't much to say at all. Or, rather, Ellen hadn't given him much chance for a defense. She didn't let up, in fact, until she seemed to remember the police were on the case. She stormed out of the room to retrieve her phone and make the call.

Left alone together, Aaron chanced a glance in my direction. I could feel the frown on my face. Could imagine the disappointment he saw on my features. It was no surprise that he hung his head sullenly in response.

I took a breath and forced the tension from my body. "Aaron…" I began carefully.

"I know already," he snapped, throwing his beanie on his desk. He unzipped his coat and threw it over the back of the chair. "Mom said everything, okay. You don't need to be involved. Why are you even here?"

Because I'm your father. Because I love you, you idiot.

I forgot, sometimes, that the teenager method of communication was very often brutal and unforgiving.

Another breath. Another careful start. "You went to a YouTube thing? What sort of event was this?"

"Just a thing that the guys from the AV club were going to." His back was to me, but I felt his eagerness to share as well as his reluctance to do so.

"Was it a concert? A seminar?"

With a sigh that resembled so many of my own, Aaron turned to me. "Just a YouTube personality. Two of them, actually. Jacksepticeye and Markiplier. They're friends so sometimes they do their meetups together."

"And you get their autographs? Is it like those comic conventions?" I was so out of touch with today's culture.

He gave me a frustrated glare. "No, Dad. It's like... they're YouTubers. They do shows. They're famous."

"Oh." I didn't have any better understanding now than before. "Are they inappropriate? Was that why your mother didn't want you to go?"

"Not really. They're just...normal. They comment on video games while they play. Mom didn't want me to go because she said I needed to get my homework done tonight since I wouldn't get any done tomorrow because of Thanksgiving and then after that you and I are doing that ski trip." He paused as he toed off his shoes. "I would have rather skipped Connecticut, but nobody asked me."

Again, that cruelty. I wondered how much of his ability to hurt me had been learned from his mother. How much he'd inherited from me. How two broken people could raise a boy to become a whole man.

Ellen had defeated me that way. She'd destroyed parts of me that I'd never have back. She'd made me bitter and cruel in return.

I vowed not to be that man to my son.

"You could have told me. I would have canceled my dinner plans tonight to take you to the event."

His eyes lifted to meet mine, surprised and curious.

"And we can cut Connecticut short. Come back Saturday night instead. If you'd like. So you can get caught up on your homework on Sunday."

"Really?" He grinned. "Thanks, Dad. That would help."

"No worries." I stepped forward to tousle his hair. It was as much physical affection as he allowed these days, and even that he often pulled away from. This time he tolerated it, and it made up for the disappointment at losing an entire day of his company.

And I couldn't say I'd been completely selfless in giving up the day with him, anyway. I had other ideas of how I wanted to spend that time.

I shut the door to the den behind me and slumped against it. "Well, that was terrible."

"Tell me about it," said Donovan, who had led me to his father's office with the promise of *"fucking escape."* He surely needed it more than I did—this was *his* parent's house, not mine. The Thanksgiving meal we'd suffered through with all its pomp and circumstance had to be more of an affront to him, and I had been quite offended.

"Are all people this terrible?" I asked, crossing over to the bar to scour for a decent alcohol.

Donovan finished cutting the cap off a cigar and stuck it between his teeth. "Rich people are."

"Thank God we aren't them," I said cheekily. "Looks like we have the option of bourbon or bourbon." I held up both overpriced bottles so he could choose.

He looked up. "The Michter. It's more expensive. We've earned it." He toasted his cigar, drew in a puff, and rotated it until the heat was evenly distributed. "You'll like this though. Illusione Epernay. It's mild the way you Europeans tend to like things."

He handed me a cut cigar in exchange for one of the

glasses I'd poured. I sniffed the foot. It smelled like coffee and cedar and, when I drew off it myself a few moments later, I detected floral and honey notes as well.

"Very nice." I sank into the oversized leather armchair and crossed my ankle over the opposite knee, letting the tension in my shoulders uncoil with the pleasant body of the tobacco. "Are all holidays with your family as awful as this one?" With more than two dozen high-class guests, the day had been filled with pageantry and performance. Much like this office with its overabundance of wood paneling and the gold-plated details. What a nightmare of a life.

"I couldn't tell you." He plopped into the rolling chair and leaned back to prop his feet on the massive desk in front of him. "I don't spend time with them for a reason."

"But now you're in the States. For good?" He hadn't given any indication that he was returning to the Japan office anytime soon, but with Donovan, you could never be too sure what his plans were.

He hesitated, either uncertain of the answer or uncertain he wanted to share it. Finally, he said, "For good."

"I'm guessing Sabrina Lind has something to do with that." I was fishing, and it was obvious. Hopefully it wasn't as evident that the person I was really curious about was Sabrina's sister, and he'd unwittingly tell me something useful.

Donovan had never been one to show his cards, though. Even years ago when I'd first met him. When he'd practically been engaged to my stepdaughter.

He wasn't eager to show them now, either. "We'll see. We'll see."

"I'm somewhat surprised she isn't here today, after that scene you made the other night. Declaring you were her boyfriend right there on the streets of Manhattan."

He gave me a sharp glare. "It wasn't a scene. It was a necessary declaration." Then, after a beat, "She's spending the day with her sister. I didn't want to interrupt."

Neither did I, which was why I was poking around for information. As she'd asked, I'd sent Audrey a text the night before when I'd gotten back to my apartment after Aaron had been found. It had been short and factual.

DYLAN: He's home. I'll talk to you tomorrow.

AUDREY: I'm so glad.<3

She'd responded right away, and I'd wondered if I'd woken her or if she'd waited up for my news. Probably the former. And still the possibility that it could have been the latter intrigued me. As did the symbols that followed. A heart, according to Urban Dictionary. Or a ballsack, depending on which definition I wanted to rely on. Either could be considered appropriate.

And yet I longed for the meaning of the heart.

I was stupid. I was raving mad. Letting my thoughts drift to her as often as they did. It was all the buildup. All the wrought-up tension between us. I needed to get laid. Obviously. It would be the only possible way to cut through the bullshit and get down to the meaning of our companionship, the pure sexuality that was the only true connection we shared.

I took another draw on my cigar as I pulled out my mobile from my jacket pocket and was surprised to find another message waiting from her. I'd forgotten I'd put it on silent for dinner.

Our T-Day reservations aren't until five, btw. You can call or text anytime before that.

I looked at my watch. It was a quarter to four. *Really?* That early, and I already needed a drink this badly?

The good news was I had time to catch her.

I set my drink down and stood up. "I, uh. Need to ring someone. Can I step out there?" I nodded toward the single French door that led to a balcony, so small it could only fit one person comfortably.

Donovan shrugged. "Doesn't bother me any. Aaron?"

I puzzled for half a second before realizing he was asking if I was calling my son. "Yes. Yes, Aaron. You understand."

Pushing open the door, I stepped quickly out into the biting cold before I could feel too guilty about the lie. Then I clicked on Audrey's name, put the mobile to my ear, and puffed on my cigar until she answered.

"You called me!" she exclaimed.

"You said I should." Had I misread her message?

"I know I did. I just didn't think you'd actually call. I expected a text, at the most."

"I've felt you come around my finger—I think we're beyond texting, don't you?"

She was silent for a moment, and I watched my breath curl with the smoke of my Epernay, anxiously wondering if I'd gone too far. Said too much. My head was filled with her was the only reason I had for my behavior. I needed to be inside her. Needed to fully have her before I could get over the distraction she imposed.

Whatever the excuse, I was preparing to deliver an apology when she said, "Ohhhh. I liked that. Is that dirty talk?"

"It's a rather lame attempt, I'm afraid. Fortunately, I was going for frankness."

She giggled, and despite the godawful temperature, I felt my cock jump at the tinkle of a sound. "So we've discovered I like frankness for sure, and possibly I like dirty talk as well. Should we try more of that to see?"

Oh, how I wanted to. Right then and there. There were a slew of filthy things I wanted to whisper to her. I wanted to tell her all the ways I meant to touch her sweet little pussy, how I would pet it and lick it and fill it up with my cum. Wanted to tell her how good her skin tasted, how drunk the scent of her made me, how the slick clench of her cunt while I'd fingered her made me ache with the need to bury my cock inside her to the hilt and fuck her until she saw stars.

But after a glance behind me at the door with its thin panels of glass separating me and my friend, I thought the dirty talk should probably wait.

"I'm hoping this call will lead to the chance for just that. Our night was cut short. I owe you a raincheck." No, that wasn't how I wanted to present that. As if she were an obligation. That was a far cry from the truth. "I'm *looking forward* to the opportunity," I amended.

She sighed wistfully. "I want to. So badly. But you have Aaron tonight through the weekend, and I leave Sunday."

"True, true. But my plans with my son have changed a bit, and I had a thought—would you be able to change your train ticket back to Delaware to something later in the day? I'm more than willing to pay for the change fee."

"Yes!" she squealed. "In fact—I didn't say anything because I didn't want to be presumptuous—but I already looked into it, and there's a train leaving at four-fifteen, and there's no charge for changing with twenty-four hours' notice. I can be at your apartment by ten-thirty in the morning."

She was fantastic. Truly.

"Then everything's settled. Sunday at my place." I glanced once more behind me and found Donovan had his eyes closed, likely sleeping off the tryptophan and dreary dinner company. I braved another comment. "I'm warning you, little girl—our lessons won't be over until my face is wet with your juices and your pussy is sore from my cock, so be prepared to learn."

She let out a noise that sounded like a shiver. "Wow, yes. I definitely like dirty talk. And now I need to go spend some alone time with my hand before I have to leave for dinner. 'Kay, thanks."

I hung up and took another draw from my cigar before opening the door, thankful that the cold prevented me having to walk in with a tent in my trousers.

"Aaron's doing good?" Donovan asked, not bothering to open his eyes at my return.

"Yes. Quite good. Excited for...for our plans this weekend." I headed back to the warm burn of the bourbon and the comfort of the armchair.

"Great to hear. I guess I won't worry about how sore your cock is going to make his pussy then."

Donovan was listening, that bugger.

Talking to Audrey had put me in such a good mood, however, I didn't have the heart to respond with anything other than a sly grin.

CHAPTER TEN

Audrey

I don't know exactly why I didn't tell Sabrina about Dylan beyond that kiss.

There were a few reasons not to, sure. After she'd rode off that night with Donovan Kincaid, they'd put their relationship on hold until they could talk, which was to happen immediately after I left town. Even with the pause, I knew she was still completely consumed with him. She didn't need to hear details of my affair. She'd fuss too much over me and neglect her own emotions like she always did. And my affair was silly compared to hers.

Or I was afraid she'd think it was silly.

Or maybe I was afraid she'd realize it really wasn't—afraid she'd realize that this thing with Dylan was really important to me in ways I couldn't explain, even to myself. Maybe I did have some daddy issues, but it was nothing I planned to discuss with my sister.

Mostly, I was afraid she'd demand those explanations. Sure, I'd tell her what I told him—that I wanted the experience, that I needed a teacher. But would I also tell her that I wanted the experience exclusively *with Dylan*? That I was attracted to him from the first words that slipped across his tongue in that to-die-for British dialect? Attracted to his tall frame and his dark eyes and that frown that rested permanently on his lips.

Would she have lectured me more about his cynicism, warning me that it was a situation that could only lead to heartache? She would have presumed I believed I could transform him.

And, no matter how much I protested, she probably wouldn't be convinced otherwise.

Most scary of all, I was afraid she would have been right. Because deep inside me there was a flicker of hope, that eternal flame that burns in hearts like mine, the same kind of light that allows zealots to proclaim tirelessly about their god. I believed, *I believed* that love fixed all. I believed in sharing that faith. Of course I wanted to convert everyone around me.

Of course I hoped I could convert Dylan, too. And that *was* silly. I didn't need Sabrina to tell me just how silly it was.

So I didn't say a word after telling her about that first kiss, and I didn't tell her I'd changed my train ticket. I worried about it silently over our last breakfast together at a cute cafe down the street. She was planning to take me to Grand Central Station to see me off, and how was that going to work? What if she saw me to security, and they didn't let me through because I was so early? What if they *did* let me through, but I couldn't sneak back out to meet up with Dylan?

"You seem distracted," she said, as we rode the elevator to her apartment to get my luggage after breakfast. "Do you have a lot of homework waiting for you?"

I did. But that wasn't on my mind. "Yeah. Homework. Finals are coming up now too."

"I should have insisted you studied more."

I threw her a glare. "No. You shouldn't have. Because you're not my mom."

She twisted her lips as though trying not to say what she wanted to say. Then she lost the battle. "Feels like it sometimes."

My immediate instinct was to take her comment personally, but I didn't want to argue with her when we were close to saying goodbye, and when I let myself think about her position, I totally understood why she'd feel she had to mother me.

"I'm sure it's a hard habit to break," I said stepping out of the elevator ahead of her. I'd meant to let it go at that, but I turned back to her instead of walking on to her door. "I'm ready to have you just be my sister. I need you to be that more than my parent these days."

She wrapped her arms around her body and frowned a moment. But then the lines around her mouth relaxed and her lips turned into a small smile. "As long as you still need me."

"I'll always need you, you psychopath."

We walked silently toward her apartment, both of us in our thoughts. Then, when she opened her door and held it open for me to go inside, she said, "I might be crazy, actually."

"Because you're going to give Donovan a chance to win back your heart?"

She kept holding it while I tugged my suitcase into the

hall. I'd left it just inside the apartment so we could just grab it and go.

"Maybe." But I could tell it was more than a maybe. That she was already back in his arms in her mind. That their impending talk was just a matter of procedure.

She was agonizing over it, though. And that's when I realized my opportunity. "Hey, you don't really need to go with me to the train station. I'll be okay getting there by myself."

"But, I want to come!"

"That's stupid and out of your way. We can say good-bye here just as easily, and then you can get to Donovan sooner."

She finished locking up and then, out of character, she pulled me into a tight hug. "I love you," she whispered, and I knew it wasn't just her way of saying thank you for letting her get to her man, but that she really meant for me to hear it.

"I love you, too." I did. More than I could ever say. She was the reason I'd made it as far as I had. She was why I hadn't turned out grim and grumpy. I'd been an orphan, and she'd upended her whole life to take care of me. She made fun of me at times, but she'd been the one who'd taught me that love wins. She'd never let me know any other way.

Downstairs, we each summoned an Uber and after another hug, we drove our separate ways. My eyes got teary, but I didn't cry like I usually did when we parted. I'd see her again in a month for Christmas, and I had a date with Dylan to distract me from how much I'd miss her.

Because I didn't have to deal with Sabrina at the train station like I'd thought I'd have to, I ended up at Dylan's building earlier than I'd planned to. I bustled into the lobby, humming "Carol of the Bells" and pulling my suitcase behind me with one hand while I wrestled with my phone's screen lock with the other. I'd just send him a text, let him know I was there already.

Obviously, I was preoccupied, which was why I wasn't paying attention and smacked right into an older guy who was coming off of the elevator. He had a solid body. Toned muscles were definitely hidden under the brick-red pullover sweater. His smelled of cinnamon and aftershave, and my belly began fluttering with butterflies before I even looked up and confirmed that the body belonged to Dylan.

His hands came up to steady me, grasping my elbows firmly. Sparks shot through my veins, and though we were about to go upstairs and get busy touching in so many other ways, I didn't want him to let me go long enough to move at all.

"Hi." I sounded shy and awkward. Not my usual self at all, which I blamed mostly on the collision, but the way he was looking at me with those liquid brown eyes didn't help.

"Hi." He gave the slightest of smiles.

Then quickly it disappeared. "Pardon me. I wasn't watching where I was going. Are you okay now? Steady enough? You aren't hurt?"

"Dad, she's fine," a thin voice grumbled.

My eyes flew to Dylan's side and collided with a teenage boy who could only be Aaron Locke. Even if he hadn't just referred to him as Dad, it was apparent the two were related. The boy had his father's height, his dimpled chin, his puppy dog eyes, his floppy brown hair.

Immediately, I stepped back, not sure how to act or

what to say. I stammered through some version of, "I'm fine, thank you." Then stood, jaw slack, as I tried to figure out what to do next. Should I zoom away without another word? Pretend we'd never met before?

Yes. That was exactly what I should do.

Instead, I stood there frozen.

Dylan wore the same panicked expression, but fortunately he seemed able to string together coherent thoughts. "Audrey, this is my son, Aaron. Aaron, this is Audrey, my…my…"

Okay, so maybe he was just as flustered as I was.

I pulled myself together and stepped in. "Your dad is my sister's boss," I explained directly to Aaron. "We somehow all ended up at dinner together the other night, and we met then."

"Weston was there as well," Dylan hurried to add, as though that might legitimize the innocence of it all.

"Right. And Donovan too," I said. Just because Donovan had shown up *after* the meal didn't make it a lie.

Of course, none of that explained what I was doing in Dylan's apartment building at the moment. I pasted on a grin and prayed silently that the kid didn't ask.

He didn't. All he said was, "Oh," barely glancing at me before throwing his gaze to the top of his shoes.

"I was just walking Aaron home," Dylan said.

His son looked up and rolled his eyes. "For the seventy-billioneth time, you don't need to. It's two blocks. I walk this street alone all the time."

Dylan's jaw tensed. "Well. We're still negotiating the walking, I suppose."

"I see," I said with a chuckle. It was the perfect opportunity to say goodbye, let them go on their way while I slipped upstairs to the apartment. I still had a key. I didn't need to be let in.

But I felt caught. Not like I'd been found out doing something I shouldn't be—though, that too—but like caught in the moment. Engaged. Drawn in.

I'd known Dylan was a father from pretty much the moment I met him. We'd talked about his son. I'd understood completely that he was a parent.

But it was totally different actually seeing him in the role.

It was the kind of thing that was hard to look away from. It felt private, but I was nosy. Like, I would see this man naked later today—if everything went as it should—and seeing him with his son seemed even more personal. Even more intimate.

I wasn't ready to walk away from it. I wanted to look a little longer. Watching the man I knew from my fantasies in his real life, as a father, was the sweetest thing I could imagine.

"I'm glad to see you made it back safely from your adventure the other night," I said, knowing I was walking a tightrope.

"You told people about that?" He threw his head back with a sigh and ran a hand through his hair, very much looking like his father.

Dylan's eyes widened, but he kept his composure. "Forgive me if stories about my son come up during small talk."

Again, Aaron rolled his eyes. "It wasn't a big deal. We just went to see a show, is all."

Dylan hadn't told me where Aaron had been. I hadn't thought it was my place to pry. Now, I asked, "A Broadway show?"

"Jacksepticeye and Markiplier had a meetup. They're YouTubers. Like, they…" Aaron trailed off, as though trying to think of how to explain them.

I helped him out. "I know who they are."

"You watch Jacksepticeye and Markiplier?" His eyes lit up for the first time since meeting him.

"Oh, no. No," I said too quickly. "I know who they are, but I don't watch them." I wasn't about to admit that I'd been at many a party hosted by someone in the art department where everyone got high and watched video-game commentators and funny things pets did.

Even not saying it, my cheeks went red. How immature was my life that I related so closely to Dylan's son? Proof that he was a grown-up, and I was just a kid myself.

"Anyway," I said, regretting the conversation. "I hope it was a good time."

"It was amazing! Had to miss a day of my ski trip with Dad, and I'm stuck doing homework all the rest of tonight, but it's not too bad."

Dylan's expression softened. "If you get done early, we'll play another game of Risk tonight."

My stomach dropped. "You're...*staying with* Aaron when you walk him home?"

He rushed to answer. "No. I'm going over later. His mother's going out, and I didn't want him to be alone."

I let out a small sigh of relief. He wasn't canceling on me, then.

"I'm alone all the time when she goes out. It's not like

I'm five."

Dylan didn't respond to his son's sass. "Ellen does go out a lot. She's quite good at...*entertaining*."

Entertaining. There was so much weight in that one word. So much history and bitterness. I'd been right when I'd guessed that she was the one to poison him, but the wound ran both deeper and closer to the surface than I'd originally thought.

"And you never entertain at all," Aaron sputtered. "A happy middle between you would be nice."

Dylan smirked. "I do too entertain. Just not when you're around. I have morals."

Aaron's cheeks pinked as he realized what his dad meant. "I mean, you could go out on a date every once in a while. You're never going to get married again if you don't."

Dylan pulled his neck back in horror. "Whoever told you I'd want to get married again?"

The disgust in his tone, the pure shock in his expression, it reminded me what the situation was between us. The reality wasn't him as a father. The reality was him as a bachelor. He was jaded. He was a cynic. He was hardhearted, and I was soft. So very soft, because somehow the truth that I'd known all along hit me with a heavy, cruel punch to the gut.

I didn't pay much attention to the rest of the conversation. I'm sure I was polite and present, then I excused myself at the next opportunity and scurried away to the elevator. As I waited for the doors to shut, I watched them continue outside, talking animatedly. Dylan never looked back once.

I bit my lip and concentrated on taking deep even

breaths until I was safely in the apartment, alone. Inside, I leaned against the back of the closed door and let out a slow, deep sigh. This was why I hadn't told Sabrina about this thing with Dylan—because I really had thought I could change him. That this little speck of an affair might make him feel something again. Something warm and wonderful.

Something warm and wonderful *for me*.

Ugh, I was such a girl. Such a romantic, pathetic, stupid girl child. My head knew better. Why couldn't my heart?

For the first time since I'd suggested this whole arrangement to Dylan, I had second thoughts. I needed to back out. I couldn't go through with this without becoming invested. He'd understand. If he didn't, he'd at least pretend like he did. He was polite like that.

And I'd learn what I liked the normal way—in a relationship with a guy who had feelings for me. The same kind of feelings I'd have for him.

My sister would have already been out the door. I felt it, firm and hard and solid behind me. It would be so easy to turn around and walk back through it, and I would—just as soon as I was sure I wouldn't start crying.

I blinked back the threatening tears, took a sniffling breath in, and tried to pull myself together. If I didn't, Dylan was going to return to find me a hot mess, and wouldn't that be the most embarrassing moment of my life?

I parked my suitcase where it was and headed further into the apartment to search for Kleenex or toilet paper. I couldn't remember where the bathroom was, though, and once I was in the living room, the glass windows called to me with their dizzy, terrifying view. I approached them cautiously, drawn to them like a tugboat being pulled at sea. I couldn't stop if I tried, even as I felt the thud thud of my heartbeat against my chest as I got closer. It was high up—so high—and looking down felt like being clutched in the fist of a giant, a fist that squeezed my torso until my lungs could no longer inflate.

I closed my eyes and the panic didn't ease, and still I felt like I was walking the edge. I was so far from it when all of this with Dylan started. I'd wanted a man who would indulge me with a no-strings sexual education. He was a man who didn't believe in strings. It had been a perfect match. We'd been fated to meet.

But I'd expected banging and dirty talk, sneaking away to meet up for something sordid and naughty. That wasn't what this had turned out to be at all. This was heartfelt conversations and seeing a magnificent man trying his best with his son. This was human and sweet and real, and I'd be lying to myself to say it didn't change everything.

So here I was now. Walking the edge. Trying with all my might not to panic and look down. Knowing there was only one sure way to stay safe.

Knowing if I didn't turn and walk away, I'd fall.

CHAPTER ELEVEN

Dylan

My heart pounded for long minutes after she left us in the lobby. My hands were sweaty, and I hadn't even put on my gloves yet. The encounter had been unexpected, and I was free-falling in the aftermath.

"She's pretty," Aaron admitted as we walked outside.

"Is she?" As if I'd been fooling anyone. As if I hadn't been simultaneously trying to tamp down my erection while she'd made casual conversation with my teenage son.

God, she was closer to his age than mine!

Did that make me a sick man to want her as much as I did?

Possibly. Probably. Definitely when I considered the kind of poison that I would be to a guileless innocent like she was, in her fashionably ripped jeans and pink-glossed lips. Colliding into her had been like crashing into sunshine. She made me feel warm in places that had been cold for oh, so long.

What did that mean that I did for her? Did she absorb the pervasive chill from my bones? Did I leave her feeling bitter, bleak, and barren?

What kind of person could take so freely from a light like her? I'd beat anyone who attempted to do the same to Aaron.

I didn't want to be that callous of a human. I refused to be.

I stopped short on the pavement and turned to my son. "I've reconsidered. You can walk as long as you go straight home. No dallying."

Aaron beamed with gratitude then scooted on his way.

And, with a sigh, I retreated back inside to do what must be done. If I was going to put a stop to this farce of a situation with Audrey, it was best to do it quick and fast. Best not to leave her waiting.

She was at the window when I stepped in. I knew she'd heard me arrive. Her head had shifted toward the sound of my footsteps, though she didn't completely turn to face me.

That made this easier.

"I think we need to reevaluate," I began.

But she spoke at the same time. "I didn't mean to come so early. I..." She pivoted in my direction. "I'm sorry. Go ahead."

"You first," I prodded, determined to remain the gentleman.

"I...just..." She pushed a lock of hair back from her face. "I got here earlier than I meant to, for which I truly apologize. I didn't think for a second I'd end up seeing you with your son." Her tone of voice suggested her line of thinking matched mine.

Why was that so disappointing?

I cleared my throat. "It does put things into perspective, doesn't it?"

She nodded ever so carefully.

"It's best, I suppose, that we figured this out now." I attempted a smile.

"It is. Definitely best." She couldn't meet my eyes. "I'll go." She lifted her chin and started toward me, toward the door.

Cold washed down the back of my neck. She couldn't stay, but I didn't want her to leave. "That's not necessary, is it? Your train doesn't depart for hours. Surely you could…"

She could…what?

"I don't think that's a good idea," she said quietly, only a meter from me now.

"No. I suppose not." I could feel the heat radiating off her body. I wanted to bathe in her sun. I wanted to bask and burn, and when she went on her way, I'd settle back into the familiarity of the gloom. Was that so wrong?

I took a step toward her, against every instinct in my body. "It was fun, though, wasn't it? As brief as it was."

"It was. It really was."

Did she just inch closer? Likely wishful thinking on my part.

"It was silly, too," she said now, and this time she definitely moved nearer. Or I did. "Thinking I could learn anything in such a short amount of time."

"I'm still convinced you didn't need to learn a single

thing." We were so close I could breathe her in now. She smelled fresh and crisp, an unusual combination of baby powder and apples. She smelled young. She smelled *too* young.

"Maybe it was just an excuse to have a new experience." She slid her tongue across her lower lip. Her gaze flicked from my eyes to my mouth.

"A new experience," I repeated.

"An amazing new experience." Her chin tilted upward. "An experience that would stay with me for a lifetime."

Someone shifted, both of us maybe, because she was in my arms suddenly, our mouths moving against each other with unbridled longing. Her hands worked eagerly at her coat, shirking it to the ground when she'd gotten it open.

I ran my nose along the slope of her neck, down the line of the shoulder that peeked from her wide cowl neck, goosebumps peppering in the wake of my journey. All thought left me. I was consumed with only her—the scent of her, the taste of her. The reality of her. I no longer cared about our age difference or the ill effect I could have on her or that I was undeserving of even a small piece of her.

I simply let the wind blow, and I let myself get carried away with it.

Never breaking our kiss, I walked her to the back of the couch, then spun her around so she could brace herself there while I enjoyed the full of her body. My hands snaked around and found their way under her gray jumper. My fingers danced over her silky, supple skin. She was soft where I was hard, inside and out, and the need to feel her everywhere, with every part of me, was desperate and unyielding.

"I feel very conflicted about these windows." I tugged

her pullover off then pinched her nipples through her bra, thrilling when she let out a delicious squeak. "I can't decide if I need to shelter you, or if I should show you off."

"Do that!" Her voice was breathless and thin, as though she were on a razor's edge the same way I was. "Show me off. Show me off!"

I lowered my hands to undo the button of her jeans, then knelt as I pulled them down as far as they'd go before becoming trapped by her boots. "Show you off it is. Everyone can watch while I eat you out."

The sound she made this time—a high-pitched, need-filled yelp—made my cock expand to its full size. I scorned the ache of it, pressing brutally against the fly of my trousers.

It distracted me, called for my attention, and the only thing I wanted to pay attention to at the moment was her, standing between me and the couch, her lace-covered ass at eye level. She'd curved her body just so, spread her legs just wide enough, that the crotch panel of her panties was front and center in my field of vision. The material clung to her shape, outlining the lips of her pussy.

She shivered as I traced the path with a solid swipe of my tongue. She was wet, and even through the cotton lining, I could taste her. She tasted sweet like pineapple and musky like bourbon, and before I'd even had my lips on her flesh, I knew she was the most delicious thing I'd ever had my mouth on.

Moving the panel aside, I tried to focus on doing some good with my lust. She'd wanted to be taught so I endeavored to show her what she liked.

"Pay attention to what I do now," I instructed her. I brushed my tongue vertically over the nub of her clit.

"That was up and down." I tilted my head and lapped horizontally. "That's side to side. And this—" I flattened my tongue and drew small circles. "Is circular. Hopefully that helps you figure out what you enjoy."

"I'm not sure. All of them," she said. "Just don't stop."

I swallowed back a laugh. There was no way I was stopping now. Burying my face in her pussy, I went down on her in earnest. I stroked and teased. I went fast, and I went slow. I sucked and nibbled, and when her legs quivered and her knees buckled, I wrapped my hands around her thighs and renewed my vigor.

She was easy to learn—her hips bucked when she wanted more, her muscles tensed when she was close. When I hit the right spot, she growled. When she was mad with desire and frustration, she begged.

She bloody begged.

"There, please, please right there," she pled like a spoiled girl. "Make it good, right there. Please, don't stop. Please, oh, please."

She was greedy, and I enjoyed gratifying her. Fucking delighted in it. Twice, I made her come. Once with only my mouth, the second time with my fingers plunging inside her as well. I could have spent all day with my face between her legs, with my tongue buried inside her cunt. If she hadn't rode through her last orgasm crying for my cock, I might have stayed on my knees long after my lower limbs had gone to sleep.

I stood, and she turned eagerly toward me, kissing me with urgency, as though she thought I might end everything right there if she didn't.

If that was truly what she thought, she was incorrect about my ability to restrain myself. I was a beast without a leash. I had no will but to devour her.

I lifted her into my arms, carrying her like a child to the bedroom.

"You aren't going to take me all the way in front of the windows? I think I'd like that," she murmured as she kissed along my jaw.

"I'm sure you would, you naughty thing. But I'm quite sure I would not." My confliction had a line, it appeared. New York City did not deserve the pleasure of her naked form.

I set her on the bed, still rumpled from the last night's restless sleep, and tugged off first one boot, then the other. She watched me, rapt, as I followed with the removal of her jeans.

"I like being undressed by you," she said, when she was only in her bra and panties. "I like how you're completely focused on me."

I couldn't not be. It was impossible to look anywhere but at her. She was exquisite and engaging. Irresistible perfection.

The wonder in her comment made me guess that no one had ever given her the attention she'd craved. What stupidity existed in her world? Boys pretending to be men, unsuitable and unworthy of such a gift as her.

I wasn't worthy either. I was a selfish vampire, feeding off her vibrant life. Even if I was damned to hell, I no longer cared.

Grabbing her bra at the space between her breasts, I tugged her forward, urging her to her knees and kissed her. Devoured her, really. It was sloppy and bruising. I wanted her lips swollen and bee-stung. I wanted her cheeks flushed and her lungs filled with my breath.

She crawled closer, her hands reaching for my belt, her mouth never breaking from mine. When she had my buckle and zip undone, she reached inside my trousers to stroke her hands up and down my bloated cock.

She pulled back and flashed me a grin. "You're big. I already know I like big."

"You're not experienced enough to know big." *Shut up,* my brain told my mouth. *You like hearing it.*

"I've only slept with two guys," she reminded me. "It doesn't mean I've only seen two cocks. And this cock…" She pulled my pants down low enough to expose the rod of flesh, red and pulsing under her gaze. "This cock is a good cock."

Fuck…this girl. She was going to be the death of me.

A bead of cum gathered at the crown, and her tongue flicked out across her lower lip.

"No," I scolded with a stern finger. "This is not for your mouth." If she were to take me that way, I wasn't sure how long I'd last. Certainly not long enough, and while I was pretty sure she made me hot enough to recover quickly, I wasn't going to make an ass of myself and prove otherwise.

Her lips turned down into an exaggerated pout. "But I've been such a good girl."

"Patience. You'll get it where you need it." I reached around to her back to undo her bra while she stroked the length of me, causing my spine to tingle and my balls to draw up. "Take my jumper off," I commanded, attempting to distract her.

"Okay, Daddy."

If she'd still been holding me when she'd said that,

I definitely would have exploded. How long had it been since I'd been with a woman? I tried to recall as she lifted my pullover up and over my head. Not too long. A matter of months. Six maybe. Not so long that I should be so near out of control.

Except that the last time I'd been with a woman, it hadn't been *this* woman. This woman hit my buttons, wound me up, got me hot like no one I could remember in a long time. Possibly ever, though that was likely an exaggeration. There was no way I was thinking rationally in a moment like this, after all.

With my torso bare, Audrey found something else to steal her attention. "Dylan...you've been hiding some seriously toned pecs." She traced the planes of my chest with the tips of her fingers, then bent forward to swirl her tongue around one very lucky nipple. When she moved to the other, she peered up at me, her eyes dark and dilated under long lashes.

Breathtaking.

That was the word for her. She stole the air from my lungs. She smothered me with her beauty, with her be-witching character. She made me heady and delirious, and if this was what it felt like to die of suffocation, I'd gladly choose this method of death anyday. Every day.

I wound my hand in the length of her hair and sharply pulled her up to face me. "Take the bra the rest of the way off. Panties too," I whispered against her lips. I kissed her, quickly. "I'm getting the condom."

I pulled open the nightstand drawer where I'd tucked a new box of condoms I'd purchased earlier in the week and retrieved a single black and gold packet. We hadn't discussed protection, but if she wanted to learn, this was something I insisted be taught—protection. Always. Without exception.

And thank God for a rubber sheath. It was the only chance I had at lasting more than a minute inside her.

When I turned back to her, she was completely naked, and I had to blink several times in order to take her in without combusting. Everything about her was pink and supple. Her puffy, well-kissed lips, the bloom of her cheeks that extended down her neck to the dusky tips of her breasts, the flush of her pussy, wet and swollen between her spread thighs.

Wet and swollen and waiting for me to fill her up.

I stripped my clothes the rest of the way off at lightning speed, and ripped open the condom packet. I was seconds from rolling it over the throbbing steel jutting from my pelvis when she spoke up.

"Can I put it on?"

The few remaining pints of blood that hadn't yet made it there, surged to my cock in a rush. "Have you ever put one on before?"

She bit her lip and shook her head.

"Then it seems this is the perfect opportunity to learn, doesn't it?"

She perched herself on the side of the bed, and I handed her the unwrapped condom. She studied it for a moment, working out which direction was up, then set it on my crown.

"I don't want it to break," she explained as she delicately smoothed it over the length of me.

She looked so innocent and naïve with her small hands wrapped around the circumference of my erection, her brows knit together in concentration. I was a dirty old man in contrast. A man old enough to be experienced at fucking by the time she was born. A man with scars worn on my aging skin and wounds that ran deeper, unseen by the naked eye. A man who knew better than to believe that sex with a woman like Audrey could ever be casual.

A man who could still crawl to shore if he tried, but didn't have the willpower to do anything except sink.

With a burst of outrage—outrage at myself for being so foolish, outrage at her for being so potently irresistible—I flipped her so she was bent over the bed, lined myself at her entrance, and drove all the way into her cunt with one blunt thrust. She cried out at the force, her body trying to jolt forward, but I dug my fingers into her hips and kept her steady and in place, ready for me to pound into her again and again. She squeaked and wriggled and grew wetter until she adjusted. Then she moaned and leaned back into the slap, slap, slap of my thighs against hers.

I wished I could watch her, wished I could scrutinize each wrinkle in her face while I stretched her and filled her and punished her pussy for being so perfect, so tight, so inexperienced. But I couldn't face her right now, couldn't look into her guileless expression while I fucked her like a well-used whore.

Because that was exactly how I fucked her—like I'd paid for the hour. Apropos since I had a feeling, when this was all said and done, there would be a price to pay. I just hoped I could afford the cost.

She was a good girl for me. She told me what she wanted with her sounds, with the rhythm of her breathing, with the way her cunt clutched at my violent stabs. She obeyed me when I demanded that she played with herself, and she stayed with the effort even as she shattered around my cock, her body convulsing with the force of her orgasm.

And I wasn't yet finished with her.

I sat on the edge of the bed and pulled her to sit on my lap. I let her ride me reverse-cowgirl style while I licked the back of her neck and pulled at her nipples. When she tired, I spanked her upper thigh then gripped her hips and moved her body for her. She came again, stuttering my name, a sound that made me wild with lust.

I couldn't resist anymore—I had to watch her face.

Again, I shifted her, laying her back onto the bed. I knelt in front of her, my knees driven wide. With my hands gripping her ankles, I spread her legs apart. She was completely on display now—the twist of her facial features, her tits as they bounced to my unrelenting tempo, her pussy as it swallowed each and every one of my cock's thrusts. This time I didn't have to tell her to touch herself, she just did, her eyes locked on me as she stroked horizontally across her clit—she was a quick learner. The best of students.

"This," she said, her gaze glossy. "I really like this. Watching you like this."

"You've had sex face-to-face before." I was always quick to anchor things in reality.

"I have. But never like this." Her thighs tightened with her oncoming climax. "I've never watched anyone watch me like you're watching me now." Her words strangled as she threw her head back and surrendered to the pleasure, but I understood them well enough.

Well enough to undo me.

I shoved in, slipping past the grip of her pussy until I was planted as deep as possible, and with a rumble of curse words, I let my orgasm wash over me, bathing me like the cold immersion of baptism, leaving me drenched and soul-stirred and new and convinced that nothing, nothing would ever be the same.

But hormones have that effect.

When I was calm and thinking straight, after we'd stroked each other's skin and bantered back and forth, after we'd each showered and washed up, I recognized the folly of the notion. Of course everything would be the same again. She was just a pretty girl—sweet and too young and sinfully wicked with her naivety. She was one of a million girls of the same mold. Maybe she was one of only a handful that would look twice at a forty-plus-year-old man, but she wasn't unique in any way.

I'd put her on a train, she'd ride off, and in a week she'd be nothing but a sordid memory to pull out when I jerked off in the shower.

"I do hope this was somewhat educational," I said when we'd reached the top of the escalators at Grand Central Station. It was as far as I intended to go. Watching her train take off from the platform was entirely too romantic for a curmudgeon like me.

"So educational." Her cheeks pinked, and I wondered exactly what it was she was remembering. "You're a very thorough teacher."

She was being kind with her flattery. Yet, I smiled and accepted the compliment all the same.

"Is anyone meeting you at the station?"

"My roommate."

She had a roommate. She had friends. She had a whole life that I knew nothing about. Didn't it feel like she knew every important thing about me? Every dull detail of my lame existence. Anything I hadn't said out loud in our brief time together could be guessed at and pieced together while she was an enigma. A puzzle I was never meant to solve.

I stopped trying. I let the cloud of mystery settle back around her and didn't ask her anything else. And when it was time for us to part, I resisted the gut-deep instinct to pull her into my arms and kiss the hell out of her, and instead, pulled her in for a polite hug.

"I suppose I have to believe in kismet now," I said, because she deserved the sentiment.

"Isn't it wonderful?"

Wonderful. Yes. It *was* some kind of wonderful.

Then I walked away, refusing to look back, even once. Refusing to do anything but move on.

I flew home to London the following day despite Weston's emphatic request that I stay for his upcoming nuptials.

"Lose another week in the States to attend your fake wedding?" I chortled. "I think not."

"What if it's not so fake?"

"Even more reason not to stay." I sounded as bitter as usual. Things did return to normal, then. As I knew they would.

A week passed. Ten days. A fortnight. Every day my thoughts turned to Audrey. Her smile haunted my dreams. Her cute quips replayed unbidden at the oddest of times. The light soprano of her voice sounded in the chorus of every Christmas carol.

I missed her. I ached for her presence. I was…

Oh, fuck.

I was *pining*.

I'd most likely never see her again, and that was best. For both of us.

But if our paths did cross in the future, if fortune deemed that we'd once more come face to face, I'd have to believe in kismet, wouldn't I? Would I believe in more, too?

Would I be ready to believe again in love?

Only fate alone could know.

SWEET FATE

*Dylan and Audrey's story concludes in Sweet Fate
(Dirty Sweet #2).*

Dylan Locke knows that pining over the young inge-
nue Audrey Lind is pointless. He can't offer her what she
wants. He definitely can't give her what she needs. Thank
goodness she's half a world away, and he doesn't have to
deal with his attraction head on.

But fate has other plans for him, and when Audrey
once again lands in his path, it's only too easy to fall back
into their easy rhythm. And then their easy banter. And of
course, each other's arms.

He tells himself nothing has changed. She still wants
forever, and he still thinks tomorrow is long enough. But
watching her search isn't as easy as he thought it would
be, and now Dylan must figure out if he's really the love
Scrooge he professes to be or if he's been Fate's willing
victim all along.

There are more dirty men in my universe.

And they all have filthy, rich love stories to share.

Dirty Duet - Donovan Kincaid

Dirty Filthy Rich Men

Dirty Filthy Rich Love

Available Now!

Dirty Games Duet - Weston King

Dirty Sexy Player

Dirty Sexy Games

Available Now!

Dirty Filthy Fix - Nate Sinclair

Available Now!

Dirty Wild Duet - Cade Warren

Coming in 2020

Also by Laurelin Paige

Visit my website, laurelinpaige.com, for a more detailed reading order.

The Fixed Universe

Fixed Series
Fixed on You
Found in You
Forever with You
Hudson
Fixed Forever

Found Duet

Free Me
Find Me
Chandler (a spinoff novel)
Falling Under You (a spinoff novella)
Dirty Filthy Fix (a spinoff novella)

Slay Trilogy

Slay One
Slay Two (fall 2019)
Slay Three (winter 2019)
Slay Four (spring 2020)

First and Last

First Touch
Last Kiss

Spark - short, steamy sparks of romance

One More Time

Ryder Brothers

Close
Want by Kayti McGee
More by JD Hawkins

Hollywood Heat

Sex Symbol
Star Struck

Written with Sierra Simone

Porn Star
Hot Cop

Written with Kayti McGee under the name Laurelin McGee

Miss Match
Love Struck
MisTaken
Holiday for Hire

About Laurelin Paige

With over 2.4 million books sold worldwide, Laurelin Paige is a New York Times, Wall Street Journal and USA Today Bestselling Author. Her international success started with her very first series, the Fixed Trilogy, which, alone, has sold over 1 million copies, and earned her the coveted #1 spot on Amazon's bestseller list in the U.S., U.K., Canada, and Australia, simultaneously. This title also was named in People magazine as one of the top 10 most downloaded books of 2014. She's also been #1 over all books at the Apple Book Store with more than one title in more than one country. She's published both independently and with MacMillan's St. Martin's Press and Griffin imprints as well as many other publishers around the world including Harper Collins in Germany and Hachette/Little Brown in the U.K. With her edgy, trope-flipped stories of smart women and strong men, she's managed to secure herself among today's romance royalty.

Paige has a Bachelor's degree in Musical Theater and a Masters of Business Administration with a Marketing emphasis, and she credits her writing success to what she learned from both programs, though she's also an avid learner, constantly trying to challenge her mind with new and exciting ideas and concepts. While she loves psychological thrillers and witty philosophical books and entertainment, she is a sucker for a good romance and gets giddy anytime there's kissing, much to the embarrassment of her three daughters. Her husband doesn't seem to complain, however. When she isn't reading or writing sexy stories, she's probably singing, watching Game of Thrones or The Walking Dead, or dreaming of Michael Fassbender.

She's also a proud member of Mensa International though she doesn't do anything with the organization except use it as material for her bio. She currently lives outside Austin, Texas and is represented by Rebecca Friedman.

Visit www.laurelinpaige.com to find out more about my books and sign up for my newsletter.

Want to be notified when I have a new release?

Text Paige to 21000, and I'll shoot you a text when I have a book come out.

51765759R00080

Made in the USA
Middletown, DE
04 July 2019